DEATH MASQUE

An unknown foreigner dies on the operating table of a
London hospital, and everything points to an error by the
anaesthetist, a former drug addict. Only one man believes
him innocent, his friend and psychiatrist, Gregor
Maclean. He suspects murder, a subtle and complex crime
camouflaged as a medical error.

Maclean is proved right when the man's wife is found
drowned. And the killer is now hunting a girl to murder
her and erase the evidence of a series of crimes committed
more than twenty years before.

Gradually, Maclean untangles the plot involving a
high-class ring of drug smugglers prepared to kill to
protect their racket and their identity, and with a
powerful ally in Scotland Yard itself.

This is Maclean at his best, in his own medical
backyard.

By the same author

Second Time Round

DEATH MASQUE

Hugh McLeave

ROBERT HALE · LONDON

© Hugh McLeave 1985
First published in Great Britain 1985

ISBN 0 7090 2229 8

Robert Hale Limited
Clerkenwell House
Clerkenwell Green
London EC1R 0HT

Photoset in North Wales by
Derek Doyle & Associates, Mold, Clwyd.
Printed in Great Britain by
Photobooks (Bristol) Ltd., Bristol
Bound by WBC Bookbinders Ltd.

ONE

Even in the lift between the ground and the sixth floors, Maclean caught a hint from the hush and tension enveloping the doctors and nurses that someone had erred and a patient had died needlessly. It set Maclean musing. Hospitals, including modern wings like this, lived in an aura of death; it permeated the concrete and chrome and white tiling, never scoured by the strongest carbolic or masked by the most potent iodoform, never erased from clothing or instruments by the hottest or steamiest autoclaves; like some virus, it pervaded the minds and clouded the faces of the medical personnel around him. Curious that among the inevitable death-roll in a five-hundred-bed hospital, he and most other staff members could detect the smell of a strange death.

No sooner had he settled in his consulting-room and run an eye down that morning's list than his secretary entered. From her stony look he guessed she had gloomy tidings and could hardly wait to unload them. Hospitals lured them as carrion did flies, these women who loved other people's misfortunes. She dumped his mail in front of him. "I suppose you've heard about Dr Rothwell," she muttered.

"Philip Rothwell? What's he done?"

"They say he mixed up the gas cylinders and gave a

patient nitrous oxide instead of oxygen, and the patient died." She almost lilted the last phrase.

"But that's not possible these days," Maclean expostulated. "When is this supposed to have happened?"

"A couple of hours ago, I think."

Maclean's eye drifted over his mail, then he picked up his list. It had four patients, two on maintenance doses of anti-depressant drugs, the third an alcoholic and the fourth a woman he had weaned off drugs. He handed his secretary the list. "Tell them I'm ill, or invent an excuse and give them an appointment with my registrar," he said.

Walking back to the lifts and waiting for the cage to take him to the basement floor and the operating theatres, Maclean debated how even somebody like Philip Rothwell came to administer nitrous oxide (laughing gas) for oxygen with all the modern, foolproof equipment they possessed; he prayed the anaesthetist had some sort of answer. Just six weeks ago, another patient had died of cerebral anoxia when Rothwell was giving the anaesthetic and although they had not proved negligence against him, it had left a bad odour. And this seemed a similar case of oxygen starvation of the brain cells. Maclean had known Rothwell for several years, both as a patient and a friend; he had worked as an anaesthetist for the psychiatrist's great friend, Professor Murdo Cameron, head of the department of surgery in a large London teaching hospital; but like many 'gasmen', Rothwell had become a drug addict which had started with his sniffing anaesthetic gases to verify them; he had quickly graduated to cocaine, heroin and LSD. Maclean had put him through a long course of psychiatric treatment but had first to use radical means to cure his addiction, stopping all his drugs except minimum doses of tranquillizers to tide him over the withdrawal trauma; after this, the psychiatrist spent months exploring the reasons for the addiction. In fact, Rothwell, an only child, had chosen his parents badly; his father, a wartime sergeant-instructor, ran his home like a drill-hall and knocked Philip's ego to pieces; his mother fussed over him, warning him of a thousand non-existent dangers, reinforcing his inferiority complex. When he struggled through medical school, he could not face setting up in practice for himself, or training to become a specialist; instead, he took the soft option, anaesthetics. It had required months of treatment before Rothwell could exist without drugs, before his scrawny, stoop-shouldered figure filled out and he could throw away his dark glasses. Maclean not only put Rothwell's ego together but found him a job as a senior anaesthetist at his own hospital.

On the operating block, a theatre sister pointed him at the second-floor staff room. There, Rothwell was sitting, dousing his umpteenth half-smoked cigarette in his coffee dregs, bleak-faced. "What happened, Philip?" the psychiatrist asked. Rothwell shook his head. "I just don't begin to understand, Gregor," he muttered. Maclean drew off two fresh cups of coffee from the machine and sat down. From Rothwell's nervous gestures and that papery complexion he could tell how fragile the man felt; but as his psychiatrist, he could not permit him to forsake all the ground he had gained over the years he had beaten his addiction. "Better tell me the whole thing as you saw it," he suggested.

In halting phrases, Rothwell described what had happened. At quarter to nine they had started a partial gastrectomy for a leaking stomach ulcer, a routine case handled by Hugh Digby, a consultant surgeon. Rothwell noticed one thing: whoever had given the patient his 'premed' must have been heavy-handed, for the patient seemed already in the second plane of anaesthesia. Rothwell had inducted the man with thiopentone, passed a tube into his windpipe to maintain anaesthesia with a mixture of nitrous oxide, oxygen and halothane. He had the right mixture for every gauge read correctly. Yet, for no reason he could fathom, the patient's breathing and pulse quickened, his blood pressure sagged, his heart began to falter and he turned a bluish colour. It appeared the more oxygen Rothwell fed him, the worse he became. Within quarter of an hour he was dead.

"So, they're blaming you for turning on the wrong taps, is that it?"

Rothwell nodded. "But I just don't see how. I checked the cylinder markings, the white and blue tubes and all the gauges." He swigged some coffee and dragged deeply on his cigarette.

"But from your own description, it looks as if the brain was starved of oxygen and saturated with nitrous oxide," Maclean remarked. "And that couldn't happen unless somebody made a mistake."

"No," Rothwell agreed. "And the engineers checked the equipment afterwards and found it worked perfectly."

"Did they test the gas in the bottles?"

"I don't know ... What do you mean?" Rothwell stared at him. "You don't think it's possible an oxygen cylinder might have been wrongly labelled and contained nitrous oxide?"

"Who can tell?" Maclean said. He suggested Rothwell might show him the operating theatre and they marched along the corridor and crossed the bridge joining the new wing to the original brick-and-tile structure of the old hospital. "How well do you know this surgeon, Digby?" Maclean asked.

"I've operated with him half a dozen times and he's all right," Rothwell said. "Even though the ulcer had burst four days ago, Digby didn't expect any trouble." Rothwell remarked that the patient seemed to have a serious accident earlier in life, for his face showed signs of extensive plastic surgery.

"You must have examined him before the operation."

"The day before," Rothwell said. "We did the usual tests – blood pressure, ECG, coagulation time and all that. Everything was within the limits for his age." As they waited for the lift to take them to the basement, he said. "He was a foreigner in his late fifties, early sixties."

"What sort of foreigner?"

"Spanish. At least that's what he spoke with his wife, though they didn't look much like Spaniards." Rothwell paused, his face pensive. "He had a good-looking daughter." Prompted by Maclean he described the man. Of light build, he had brown eyes and dark hair. Rothwell remembered the face best. Some plastic surgeon had evidently worked for months to rebuild the jaw which had been broken in several places; he had also grafted skin on to the cheeks and forehead. "Whoever did it hadn't made much of a hash of it," Rothwell said. "It looked to me like an accident or a burns job. I imagined he'd been in a crash and his car had caught fire, that sort of thing.

"How did you get through to him if he spoke only Spanish?"

"I got nowhere with him or his wife. I had to buy his daughter a coffee in the canteen and get her to answer what questions I had about his medical history."

'How old is she?"

"I'd say 20, 21?"

"Any idea what she does?"

"From the little she said I guessed she was over here studying at London University."

"Did you get their address in London?"

Rothwell shook his head.

"Do you know who referred them here?"

"Search me," Rothwell said. "I only came into the case a couple of days before the op."

They got out of the lift and stepped along to the older Number One operating block in the original building. Rothwell pushed through the Perspex swing doors of Theatre B. To Maclean, it appeared like any of the older operating rooms he had seen, with an adjustable surgical table surrounded by instrument trolleys, a portable X-ray machine and glass-fronted shelves set in the green tiling to house drums of sterile clothing, metal boxes of surgical instruments, suture thread and needles, drugs. Gazing at the clutter of equipment, Maclean meditated on the difference between this and the New Block theatres where everything was built-in and looked tidy, where all the gases were piped from a central pool and the tubes were coloured to denote oxygen, nitrous oxide and suction. And they had patent nozzles. Over there, Rothwell could never have mistaken one gas for another.

Maclean made for the anaesthetic trolley. Despite refinements, it did not differ much from the old Boyle's Machine he had used as a fifth-year student to give the gas for Murdo Cameron in the university's surgical unit during their days at Edinburgh. "It hasn't been touched as far as I know, except by the engineers," Rothwell muttered. Maclean let his eye wander over the various gauges that monitored blood pressure, heart-beat and respiration before turning to the two main cylinders feeding oxygen and nitrous oxide into the face mask, or the endotracheal tube. Rothwell levered both the nozzles of the gas bottles free, pointing to the bayonet sockets into which they fitted. "You see, how can anybody go wrong?" he asked. "These sockets are different sizes, one for oxygen, the other for nitrous oxide. And I'd swear on my oath that's the way they were when we operated this morning. Even the bottles are marked for the different gases."

"All that's fine," Maclean agreed. "But say somebody changed the nozzles on the cylinders and repainted the markings. Would you pick that up on your monitoring system?"

Rothwell shook his head. "They're only pressure gauges and would tell me I was giving oxygen when the patient was really getting nitrous oxide." He gazed at Maclean, frowning. "But if anybody did that it would mean they were trying to kill the patient."

"Or meant to kill you – professionally," Maclean muttered. He reached into a baggy pocket, produced an ebony snuffbox, took a pinch of strong snuff, in-haled this and blew his nose into a polkadot handkerchief. Since his own cure for alcoholism fifteen years before, he had made no other concessions to addiction. Pocketing the handkerchief, he fixed Rothwell with his blue eyes. "Philip, I've got a couple of questions to ask you. Think before you answer. Recently, you had another death on the table that people suspected was your fault, for much the same reasons as they suspect you now. Do I have your word you're not back on drugs?"

"I haven't taken anything stronger than coffee or aspirin for five years," the anaesthetist protested.

"All right, I believe you even if you might have a job to convince the board of governors." Maclean walked to the swing doors and glanced through the port-hole windows along the empty corridor. "Think hard before you answer this one – have you got any enemies in this hospital?" Rothwell reflected for several minutes then shook his head. Maclean looked at him. "Nobody after your job? No ward or theatre sister you've been having fun with and who thought it was serious and now wants to get her own back?"

Again Rothwell hesitated, shaking his head though more dubiously. "Well, there is somebody – but no, she'd never do a thing like that," he whispered.

"Who's she?"

"It's a theatre sister who – well, she thought I was in love with her and she said she was in love with me and – well, maybe she thinks I did her dirt."

"What's her name?"

"Sister Anne Maxton. She's on the New Theatre block and works with Hugh Digby and his registrar in their firm as well as doing private work for a couple of other surgeons."

"Was she here this morning?"

Rothwell nodded. "She set up the theatre for the operation and assisted Digby and his registrar, Linton."

"You say she thinks you stood her up. Did you?"

Rothwell paused a moment then shrugged. "I suppose so, but then a lot of people have before me. I'd say she's moved around and slept around a lot."

"Who's sleeping with her now?"

"I wouldn't know. I've only been with this firm a couple of weeks on loan."

"And you? Who's your new playmate?"

"Nobody on the operating block," Rothwell murmured. "I was friendly with a nurse in Obstetrics."

"And I suppose she's younger and prettier than Sister Maxton and probably didn't allow her to forget the fact when they met around the hospital or in the nurses' canteen," Maclean said.

Nervously, Rothwell plugged the two tubes from the bottles of gas into their sockets; he turned on each tap and sniffed the gases in the way anaesthetists do. He glanced at the psychiatrist. "Anyway, Anne Maxton would never dream of landing me in it like that – and I know her well enough to say she'd never kill off a patient at the same time. You can't believe that, Gregor."

"I didn't say a thing," Maclean murmured. He was studying the bayonet sockets into which the anaesthetist had clipped the two nozzles, running his finger round the brass fittings and screwing up his eyes to examine them more closely. "I suppose they would clear the theatre when the patient died," he remarked.

Rothwell nodded, then thought of something. "Hugh Digby normally operates in the New Block, but all those theatres were working, so they'd fixed this op in Theatre A."

Maclean stared at the stencil on the door. "But this is Theatre B."

Rothwell nodded. "We couldn't use Theatre A this morning because the battery of operating lamps went on the blink when Maxton and her staff tried them – so we moved in here."

"Does that happen often – lights on the blink?"

"Only once before in my five years here, and it was the same thing – a burnt-out fuse."

"Was this the only theatre available when you discovered the lamps didn't work?"

"I'd think so," Rothwell muttered. "In fact I'm sure the other four rooms in this block were all operating when we started quarter of an hour late."

"When Digby and his firm moved back into Theatre A after the operation on this foreigner, did anybody occupy this theatre? I mean, was another position scheduled?"

"I don't think so."

Maclean accompanied the anaesthetist to the staff room and left him with the injunction to say as little as possible to anybody about the incident, and to admit nothing. Let them prove malpractice or negligence against him if they could. On the pretext that he had mislaid his snuff-box in the operating theatre, Maclean ambled back along the corridor and went down in the lift to the basement. Back in the theatre, he ran the anaesthetic trolley into a corner where he hoped nobody would spot him; he hoped, too, the surgeon who operated there would forgive him for misusing the bulldog clamp he borrowed from an instrument tray. Around the flat edge of the clamp he wrapped two thicknesses of handkerchief; this covered flange he inserted into the slots of the two bayonet sockets of the trolley and unscrewed them. He was right. Those clever fellows who fancied they had devised a fireproof method of preventing patients from receiving laughing gas instead of oxygen should have altered the sizes of the screws as well as the sockets. It was so easy to substitute these sockets. Without a powerful magnifying-glass he could not confirm if someone had recently unscrewed them and perhaps it would have proved nothing in any case; but such a trick would work just as well as doctoring and swopping the gas cylinders. When he had replaced the sockets, he returned to his own consulting-room and sat there going over various possibilities in his mind. He had no more than a smell in his nose, not much stronger than the hint in the lift when he had entered the hospital; but it told him that perhaps both Philip Rothwell and the unfortunate patient in Theatre B were victims of someone who wanted to destroy the anaesthetist's career or the patient's life. Or both.

TWO

Before tackling Rothwell's problem, Maclean had one of his own. He had to clear his lines with the girl who shared his life, looked after his well-being and Harley Street practice and vehemently opposed anything that distracted him from his patients and sent him chasing this or that medical conundrum, even if it did hint of crime. Without Deirdre O'Connor he would never have created a Harley Street practice in the first place. He had met her when she was a senior nurse in a clinic for alcoholics and he had hit rock-bottom as a drink addict who had killed his wife in a car accident and had narrowly escaped being struck off the medical register. Deirdre had nursed him through weeks of aversion therapy, another term for torture chamber, doping him with an alcohol antagonist like apomorphine and feeding him whisky until the sight, smell and taste of alcohol revolted him. He would have given up but she had forced him to hang on, caring for him first out of duty, then sympathy and finally love. Now, her practical sense and medical experience were vital in running his practice; indeed, Deirdre had a hand in choosing many of his patients and often her Irish intuition or sixth sense unearthed some vital fact or trend from the taped or typed records of patients' sessions with Maclean. In some of the strange cases he had solved outside his practice, he had relied on her spaewife clairvoyance to straighten out his own thinking. In short, he needed her.

But had he rung her at the practice and laid the bald facts before her, she would have pooh-poohed the suggestion of foul play, accused him of malingering and pulled his ears back to his afternoon list. However, like many women, Deirdre had to imagine that most if not all the best ideas came from her. So, Maclean reasoned that if the anaesthetist called Harley Street and hinted there was a conspiracy to destroy him, then threw himself on Deidre's mercy, she might then make the running. Maclean disliked using such subterfuges but he could not move without her blessing; he scripted the dialogue for Rothwell, briefed him thoroughly, then eavesdropped while he spoke to Deirdre, almost begging her help to win the psychiatrist round; Rothwell declared he did not want to make a direct approach and risk a rebuff; Maclean would assume he was hooked on drugs again; but she could talk her boss round. Deirdre sounded flattered. Within minutes, the phone in Maclean's office rang. Deirdre apologized for disturbing him, then said Philip Rothwell was in deep trouble; with great indignation, she said they were accusing him of something not far short of manslaughter.

"Yes, I heard some talk about that this morning," Maclean murmured. "Pity about poor Philip, mavournin."

"What do you mean, pity?" she cried. "Are you one of those in that slaughter-house who think he's guilty before he's had half a chance to defend himself?"

"Hmm, you've got to admit he's a former addict."

"So are you," she countered.

"I mean, they'll assume the worst," he said, then added in a cool voice, "But anyway, what more can they do than fire him with a reprimand?"

"And you know well enough that'll be the end of Philip," she said, anger broadening her Irish brogue. "He's a patient of yours, or have you forgotten?"

"No – I suppose he's a patient," Maclean muttered. "What do you suggest we do, mavournin?"

"You can at least go and see him and find out what went wrong in that operating theatre."

"But I'm way over the head in patients."

"Philip's worth more than all your hospital neurotics put together," she snapped. "Hand them over to your registrar and let him do some work for a change."

"Very well," Maclean said, grudgingly. "But if I agree to see Philip, would you come over and give me a hand to sort out his little problem?"

"Of course," she said and banged the phone down, unaware he had led her by her freckled nose to act contrary to all her previous instincts.

Now Maclean had a free hand and could therefore concentrate on the problem. Yet, he must tread warily. Not only was the hospital conducting its own inquiry into the patient's death but within a week, Her Majesty's coroner would hold an official inquest, calling a dozen or so witnesses to help him and his jury judge where the blame lay. More important, if Maclean's hunch meant anything and someone in the hospital had murdered a patient, either for a specific motive or to have Rothwell accused of negligence, then that someone would be watching his back against snoopers like Maclean; and a murderer ingenious enough to plan what might have passed for a perfect crime would soon fasten on him if he started quizing or probing among Digby's staff who had assisted at the operation.

However, ward staff who had to cope with hundreds of relatives, friends and strange visitors every week might show less reluctance to give him information, so he would begin on the ward. When Rothwell had verified the man's name, Miguel Contreras Heredia, and the number of the private room he had occupied on the fourth floor, Maclean took the lift down, arriving just before eleven as the staff were relaying each other for their coffee break. Without being spotted he slipped into the room Señor Heredia had left alive earlier that morning, closing the door behind him. Already they had stripped the bed and removed the bathroom towels and mat, but he could see the cleaners had not yet swabbed the floor and walls. However, someone had emptied the waste-paper baskets in both the room and bathroom. This he deduced from seeing the torn scrap of envelope they had overlooked on the bedside table. Surely a man facing a serious and perhaps fatal operation left more of a legacy than an envelope with a Spanish stamp and a hospital address on it. Wrapping the torn scraps in his handkerchief, he thrust them into his pocket. They had also left Heredia's medical chart hanging on the end of the bed. A glance at this told him that the Spaniard was 61, had a sound heart and lungs though he suffered from mild hypertension and anaemia, needed sedatives and sleeping-pills and had required four pints of blood on admittance four days ago. That morning he had been given premedication of pethidine and atropine. Maclean was standing, chart-board in hand, memorizing the details when the door burst open and young woman in theatre sister's uniform stepped into the room. Her wide eyes glared at him. "Who are you and what are you doing in this room?" she cried.

Maclean took in her grim grim face and tight lips and noticed she was clutching an outsize set of surgical clamps like a truncheon, as though poised to strike; he was deliberating whether to sidestep or launch a frontal assault. With such a woman he had little option. "Sister, I happen to be the consulting psychiatrist on the staff of this and several other hospitals and I have a right to be here. May I ask who you are and what you want?"

That wrong-footed her and she reddened. "I'm sorry, Doctor, I didn't recognize you. I'm Sister Maxton and I have several patients on the surgical ward, including the man who occupied this room. Were you interested in this patient?"

Maclean noted that she acted anything but sorry and the flush spreading over her fair skin stemmed from anger rather than remorse, and her eyes, green as glacier-water, paraded over his face and bulky figure and baggy suit and narrowed with disbelief. "One of my patients was under observation with Mr Cranmer, the neuro-surgeon, and has just had a brain scan and I came to see him. They informed me he was in this room."

Sister Maxton suddenly smiled and the tension drained from her face. "But you're on the wrong floor," she said with a laugh. "Neurosurgery's on the fifth floor."

"Where is this?"

"Ward B ... on the fourth floor."

"These damned lifts," Maclean grumbled. "I must have put my finger on the wrong button. I'm an idiot, Sister, and I apologize." He slung the medical chart back on its hook. Miss Maxton was still smiling though he noticed those cold, green eyes did not reflect the smile; she still did not entirely believe him and was wondering exactly what he was seeking in that too-empty room. Now he realized what had attracted Philip Rothwell to her; under her fan-shaped nurses' cap she had soft, wavy blond hair, a face both pretty and intelligent and a *svelte* figure. But he did not like the idea of those sea-green eyes boring into his back as he strode along the corridor, cursing his imprudence and the fact he might have fired her suspicions.

Returning to his office, he found Deirdre waiting for him. She listened while he explained what Rothwell had told him and his own little bit of sleuthing; she agreed with his theory that someone in the hospital had plotted to blacken the anaesthetist. "It must be one of the staff on the ward or in the operating theatre," she suggested.

"Very probably," he conceded. "But dozens of other people must have known about that operation. It would have been posted by admin."

"I'll get the details," Deirdre said.

"Don't make your inquiries too obvious," Maclean cautioned, described his brush with Sister Anne Maxton. "Find out what you can about the patient, his relatives, if they've collected his belongings and what's going to happen to the body."

When Deirdre had disappeared along the corridor Maclean picked up his own phone and rang the hospital workshop in the basement. Within ten minutes Bob Monk had appeared in his office. Head of the engineering staff, Monk would have done anything for the psychiatrist and not only because he had treated two of his relatives for nervous illness. In Monk's book, trick-cyclists came in bastard sizes with normal ones as scarce as white crows; this Scotsman might look like two bags of spuds standing on top of one another, but he had no side and did not go in for bullshit like some of the other consultants in black jackets and sponge-bag pants. Monk's young nephew still raved about the sight-seeing tour Maclean had done with him, starting at the Tower and finishing at Regent's Park zoo, to help cure his crowd phobia. Monk came forward to shake the psychiatrist's hand. "What's the problem, Dr Mac?" he asked.

Maclean told him about Rothwell and his own detective work; then he listened as the engineer described how he, himself, had examined the trolley after the operation that morning and found nothing amiss. Swearing Monk to secrecy, Maclean confided his hunch that someone might have tampered with the gas trolley. After reflection, the young engineer conceded that anybody could have swopped the fitments and changed the bottles around; but if they had changed the bottles, they'd have had to substitute normal cylinders afterwards since his staff had checked those from the machine and confirmed they contained the gases marked. "We can check to see if the fitments have been tampered with," he proposed.

"No point," Maclean replied. "Anybody contriving to change those screws did it without leaving any trace." Levering himself to his feet, he suggested Monks show him the fuse-boxes in the operating theatre blocks. Down they went to the basement and along to the old block where the boxes were placed; Monk explained how these were connected to the various circuits and to the main monitoring unit in his his headquarters. He flicked open the box for the old-block theatres and pointed to the fuse that had blown several hours ago.

"You mean, this morning?" Maclean queried, his face puzzled.

Monk nodded. Every circuit in the hospital came up on the display panel in his headquarters if a fault developed. Some essential equipment such as iron lungs, kidney machines, heart-lung machines and mechanical respirators had double circuits and their own power unit which switched on automatically in case of a mains failure or a blown fuse.. That panel was manned round the clock.

"So you must have logged the exact minute that fuse blew," Maclean said.

"At eight forty-nine precisely."

"Just after the theatre staff entered to prepare the place for the operation," Maclean mused aloud. "That means somebody short-circuited the lamps …"

"No, we'd have picked that up when we carried out our routine checks on the circuit," Monk objected.

"Who replaced that fuse?"

"Johnson, the duty electrician."

"Would he keep the blown fuse?"

"No, we never do. Why?"

Maclean ran his finger along the array of fuses, all cartridge type and the same size. "Let's argue I wanted those operating lights to fail this morning. I'd choose a three-amp fuse for that battery of theatre lamps which require something like fifteen amps. As soon as anybody switched on the lights, they'd blow within seconds. And I'd know that, in case there might be a more serious electrical fault endangering some patient's life, your men would call for a complete check of the theatre and it would be evacuated."

"That's exactly what happened," Monk admitted.

"The fuse could have been switched the night before," Maclean continued. He reflected for a moment. "Would Johnson have looked at that fuse?"

"Give me a minute," Monk said. Stepping to the middle of the corridor, he picked up the intercom phone and spoke to someone in the control room. He returned, nodding his head. "You got it right, Dr Mac – everything but the fuse resistance. It was five amps, and Johnson thought one of his pals had boobed by choosing the wrong fuse, so he said nothing about it."

"Don't you, either," Maclean said, thanking the engineer.

Deirdre returned to his office with the notes she had picked up in Records. Miguel Heredia had Spanish nationality and a San Sebastian address on his passport; he had a wife, Carolina, who had just collected his effects, and a daughter, Maria. They had given a small hotel in Notting Hill Gate as their London address. A general practitioner in the same district, a Dr Cardew, had treated him and ordered an ambulance from the East End Hospital.

"Why this hospital?" Maclean interrupted. "There are at least a dozen hospitals nearer Notting Hill than this one. Did he know anybody here?"

Deirdre shrugged her ignorance. She went on to say the hospital was holding its own inquiry into the death and the coroner's inquest would take place in a week's time.

"And the autopsy?" Maclean asked.

"This afternoon. That's being done by Hopkins, the constultant pathologist," she said.

"Did they say what the family wanted done with the body afterwards?"

"His daughter asked about cremation, so they think he's being cremated and his ashes flown back to Spain."

"But they've given his religion as a Roman Catholic," Maclean said, pointing to her notes. "When did

Catholics start going in for cremation?"

"Maybe they haven't got the money to fly a coffin back for burial," she suggested.

"No, there's some other reason," he said, shaking his head. "They had the money to get here, the daughter's studying here. And I'd say they must have paid Digby a fee and had to meet their hospital expenses – the room, lab tests, X-rays and so on."

Deirdre looked at him, her blue eyes puzzled. "You think, then, they might have chosen the Spaniard intentionally?"

"I don't know," Maclean said. "Could be. But it might have been somebody who didn't care who he killed providing Philip Rothwell was giving the gas."

"It was obviously somebody in the hospital in that case."

Maclean nodded. From his desk drawer he produced a list. "Philip jotted down the names of everybody he has worked with in five years he's been here. Most of them knew about his drug problem and his previous so-called accidents."

"But if they murdered ..." Deirdre ran a finger down her freckled nose. "That could only be a woman," she exclaimed.

"You're probably right, mavournin," Maclean murmured, recalling Anne Maxton's cold, green eyes. Like Deirdre, he inclined to the theory that someone wanted to wreck Rothwell's life; it seemed too far-fetched to think of a doctor or a member of the medical personnel devising such a subtle plot to murder some Spaniard who had arrived for an ulcer operation; they could have arranged to kill the man in so many other ways. Yet, some niggling intuition whispered that a link existed between the Spaniard's death and the plot to ruin Rothwell.

THREE

Wheeling the trolley into place and switching on the fluorescent lighting, the morgue attendant drew back the linen sheet and glanced at Maclean, who signified he had the right man; then he left the psychiatrist to contemplate the face and naked body of Miguel Contreras Heredia. For some reason, Maclean had expected someone aged 61 with a stomach ulcer to have a lined face and grey or grizzling hair; but against the marble pallor of the features, the hair shone jet-black. However, at the hair roots, he discerned a faint discoloration, enough to convince him that Señor Heredia dyed his hair, which was either fair or white; this he confirmed by looking at the dead man's chest and pubic hair. Heredia's face looked younger, too. Only round the eyes and upper lip had age wrinkled and creased the skin, but because the smooth skin of his cheeks, chin and forehead had come from elsewhere; even on that white veneer of death, the grafts showed a different texture, and bristle had grown only on the upper lip and a few other patches. Maclean saw that much of this skin must have been taken in paper-thin Thiersch grafts from the stomach and the inside of the thigh; it looked, too, as though the jaw had been broken and remodelled. When alive, this face must have had a sort of timelessness conferred on it by the plastic surgeon with that smooth, hairless skin. One thing struck the psychiatrist as curious: the nose betrayed no sign of having been burned or fractured. In most accidents, that organ suffered some damage. Evidently Señor Heredia had false teeth, upper and lower, and these had been removed to leave the face looking small and compressed by the thong supporting the lower jaw. With a finger, Maclean flicked open one eye, hoping that death had not begun to change or leech the colour; instead of widely dilated pupils, he noticed both eyes looked normal though they glittered with a sterile, unnatural light. Bending over, he realized Señor Heredia wore contact lenses and these seemed to have been cleverly tinted to give the appearance of brown irises. Maclean speculated about he original colour of the eyes. Blue most likely, since the hair was fair. Keeping watch on the attendant's cubicle in the foyer, he moved round to the side of the body; from a pocket, he slipped his office stamp-pad and a sheet of paper and quickly impressed the dead man's right-hand thumb and fingers on the pad then on the paper. When he had scribbled several notes in his diary about the corpse, he draped the sheet over it and went to thank the attendant. As Maclean was leaving by the main door, a woman in her late thirties, early forties, pushed past him and went inside; she stopped to whisper something to the attendant who escorted her into the interior of the morgue. Observing from the door, Maclean saw him pull back the sheet from Heredia's body and leave the woman there.

"Who is she?" he whispered as the man returned to his cubicle.

"Says she's a relative," he replied.

Maclean watched the woman kneel and pray by the body. He stood, waiting, and when she emerged from the door, he accosted her. "Excuse me, madam, are you a relative or friend of Señor Heredia?" he asked.

"I am ..." she began, then checked herself. She said, slowly, in Spanish, *"No hablo y no comprendo inglès."* Barging past him, she made for the lift. He caught up and placed himself between her and the door. He held out his professional card. *"Señora, hé acquì mi carta. Tomele per favor en caso que yo puedo ayudarla."*

Her eyes widened on hearing him speak Spanish; but she drew herself up, stared scornfully at the card he proffered then shook her head. Before he could stop her, she had turned and run upstairs by the side of the lift; he could not hope to hoist his bulk quickly enough to catch her slim figure disappearing round the bend in the stairs. So that was Heredia's wife. She spoke English but obviously did not want to let on. And those blue, Nordic eyes and blond hair looked anything but Spanish. What sort of eyes and hair did the daughter have? He wondered about that as he took the lift to the admin floor and ran off several duplicates of the fingerprints he had taken. From his office, he rang Detective-sergeant John Pearson and offered him a snack lunch at a pub in Victoria near Scotland Yard.

Maclean got there first and ordered a smoked-salmon sandwich with his normal tipple, tonic water. A few minutes later, the huge figure of Pearson dumped itself on a bar stool beside him; he bought himself a pint of bitter and half a chicken with salad. Six feet three inches in his socks, Pearson had a craggy, knocked-about face with a lop-sided chin, broken by a couple of thugs during his three years on the beat. He had graduated in one of the worst London districts, Southwark, ruled by mobs like the Krays and Richardsons. As a legacy of those days, he still sported chiv marks on his right cheek from tussling with men using open razors. Although burly as well as big,

Pearson moved lightly and quickly and, in his younger
days, had won the Metropolitan light-heavyweight
boxing championship; that trophy and others lay in an
attic trunk with the police medal for bravery, awarded
for tackling and disarming a gunman holding up a local
post-office. What Pearsons lacked in brilliance he
made up in loyalty and resolution. Maclean and he had
first met during the trial of Neil Archer for murdering
a nymphomaniac socialite; the psychiatrist had tried,
vainly, to persuade the defence to plead guilty but
insane and thus save Archer from the gallows. Pearson
had helped him get the evidence of Archer's previous
crimes and they had become friends. The detective had
called on the psychiatrist's experience to help him
solve several crimes involving psychopaths and
paranoid personalities. Now Maclean was asking for
aid from someone he could trust; and he knew Pearson
paid for all his own food and drink, settled his betting
losses and matched this honesty with discretion.
Without emphasizing his suspicions, Maclean outlined
the Heredia story as it had unfolded that morning;
only then did he put his own construction on the facts.

"Wait a minute, Dr Mac," Pearson interjected. "If
you think there's a crime involved, I should be
informed officially. You know that."

"But the only crime is medical negligence, and you'd
have to build Scotland Yard twice over if you checked
on every dubious hospital death," Maclean countered.
"You know what they say about medicine – it's an art
founded on conjecture and improved by murder."

"All right, but you think this may be a murder."

"It's no more than a supposition, but I believe the
story as Rothwell, the anaesthetist, tells it. And I think
the blown fuse is too much of a coincidence."

"Any idea who might have done it?"

"Somebody who knows their medicine. Somebody who knows Rothwell's weakness and background. Somebody pretty clever."

"And the motive?"

"Take your pick. Either to destroy Rothwell or murder Heredia or both. But whichever one they were aiming at it's still murder."

"No question, if your hunch is right," Pearson conceded. He ordered himself another pint, a hunk of Cheddar and a fistful of roll and ate and drank as he debated what Maclean had told him. Finally he said, "How are you going to prevent them from destroying the evidence – burning this dago?"

"How can I?" Maclean asked. "I don't want to alert everybody in the hospital including the criminal. And I don't want to hint to the family that it might be murder rather than malpractice."

"I know Thurgood, the coroner for that district. If you like, I can bite his ear to hold up the cremation certificate."

"It would help," Maclean said. He passed the information Deirdre had collected and one copy of the fingerprints. "I took these prints off the body this morning just in case they're in your files," he explained. "I thought Señor Heredia had gone to such trouble to change his appearance that he might have done something wrong when he was younger."

"How long ago would you say he'd had this plastic surgery?"

"Impossible to say. Those grafts don't grow hair or show worry or take on character like your face or mine. But at a guess fifteen, twenty years."

Pearson pocketed the papers. "I'll have somebody in Criminal Records Office put these on their computer," he said. "In fact, I'll do better, I'll get CRO to ask

Interpol to check with its Paris headquarters in case an international alert went out on Heredia."

"It may not be his name."

"They've other ways of identifying people."

"How long will it take?"

"A day or two for our files with so little to go on. A week for Interpol if they have to ask their Madrid office." Pearson hoisted himself off the bar stool, muttering that he wished he had something interesting like this Heredia case; he had to get back to a Hatton Garden jewel robbery, a hit-and-run accident and a mugging. Maclean accompanied him to Scotland Yard, then continued through the back streets, past Wellington Barracks to St James's Park. It was one of those still, limpid spring days with a few feathery clouds overhead, their shadows drifting across the lake. He sat on a bench, crumbling the handful of bread he had pinched and throwing it to the swans and ducks, letting his thoughts ripple over the bits and pieces of the conundrum. An anaesthetist was blamed for a patient's death. But a strange patient looking like a man disguised. With a scared wife who thought herself threatened. Six people had begun that operation and at least one of them, Sister Anne Maxton, had a motive for plotting Rothwell's downfall and disgrace; others realized how vulnerable the anaesthetist was. But surely she would have involved somebody else! Digby? Maclean knew nothing about the ENT surgeon, but everyone reckoned him a good operator, if a bit erratic. Roger Linton, his surgical registrar, seemed to have no motive and no link with Rothwell or his circle; both remaining theatre sisters, Elizabeth Maitland and Barbara Grace, he regarded as extras for little part in the action. What did he really have? No more than suspicions of murder hinging around a blown fuse and switched gas bottles. However, since malpractice and negligence formed part of the normal hospital pattern, he would not get much further than suspicions unless Pearson or someone else came forward with new facts.

He had two more calls to make. Strolling across the park to The Mall he hailed a cab which took him to Notting Hill and the cul-de-sac of Victorian houses where the Gatehouse Hotel lay. From the outside, the twin mansions forming the hotel looked shabby, their stucco crumbling in places, the sign lettering bleached by London's acid atmosphere; inside, the small and dingy lounge smelled of stale tobacco and stew from the dining-room and kitchen beyond. A blowzy, cinder-blonde woman, her breath heavy with gin, answered the bell. "I'd like to see Señora Heredia," Maclean said.

"Who'd you say?" He repeated the name.

"Nobody of that name 'ere," the woman wheezed.

"Well, whatever she was called. A Spanish lady who came with her husband, a sick man who had an operation and died."

"Oh, that one." She dragged deeply on her cigarette. "You're the second one after her this afternoon. She left here before noon as though she'd found a dead rat in her bedroom." Maclean watched her hyperthyroid eyes parade all over him and felt her hostility. "You a friend?" she asked.

"No," Maclean, evenly. "It's a professional call."

"What kinda professional call?"

"A private one," he said, smoothly. "Did Señora Heredia leave an address for mail?" A twitch of her head signified, No. "Did she mention where she was going?" This time, the women did not even respond but fixed her blood-shot eyes on Maclean's face. He produced a small diary and pretended to consult some notes, aware she was watching him. "She and her husband arrived – let's see – just nine days ago, wasn't it? You must know who booked them into your hotel."

"No, I don't, mister. I wasn't here, and my receptionist girl's on her day off." Ambling round his side of the desk, she went to the front door and held it open, pointedly. "Now if you've finished your quiz game, I've got some work to do," she said.

Maclean walked down Westbourne Grove thinking there was a lady either too deeply embroiled, or bent on minding her own business. At a tree-lined crescent he turned and continued until he came to a house with a brass plate on one of the portico columns. It read: Dr J Anthony Cardew. MB Ch.B. A girl answered his ring, looked at her watch and said, "Sorry, doctor hasn't started his evening surgery yet – not for another half-hour."

"It's a personal matter," Maclean replied. "I'm a colleague. It's about a patient." He identified himself with a medical card which she scrutinized before admitting him into a waiting-room with a few wooden chairs, a table piled high with dog-eared magazines and a flabby, dusty rubber plant by the window. Within minutes the surgery door opened and Dr Cardew beckoned him inside, offered a chair and placed himself behind his desk. He had bald hair, thick specs and dirt under his fingernails of his large hands. Maclean introduced himself, then said, "I'm trying to trace Señora Heredia."

"Heredia?" Cardew screwed up his eyes behind his thick, rimless glasses and looked puzzled. "Do I know a Señora Heredia?"

"I'm sorry," Maclean murmured. "I was under the impression you sent her husband to the East End

Hospital for surgery and might therefore know his wife."

"Ah, yes! Now I remember," Cardew said, his voice relieved. "He wasn't my patient. I was merely called by the hotel and found this Spaniard with a perforating ulcer. I had to phone for an ambulance and hospitalize him."

"But why the East End, on the other side of the city?" Maclean queried. "Did he know somebody there?"

Cardew thought about that for a good moment, drumming with a chased silver paper-knife on the table. "It was a holiday Sunday," he said in a musing voice. "There was a run on ambulances and when I'd phoned two or three, I contacted the emergency centre and presumably they referred him to the East End."

To Maclean, that rang phony, but he let it pass. "Did you see his wife?" he asked.

Cardew nodded. "She was in the hotel room and I'm pretty sure she accompanied him in the ambulance."

"You haven't seen her since?"

Cardew shook his head. He stopped drumming. "If it's not indiscreet, why all the questions?"

"You didn't know Heredia died on the table?"

"No – when?" Cardew now looked perplexed and worried.

"This morning, just after nine."

"Were you a friend, Dr Maclean?"

"A family friend," Maclean said. "But I've been away and didn't know they were in London until I heard about Heredia's death." He rose, murmuring his thanks and the general practitioner showed him to the door. Maclean walked to his own flat, ten minutes away on the Bayswater Road. Those two interviews had hardened his suspicions about Heredia's death. That painted, gin-scented creature in the hotel had not called Dr Cardew by accident; and from Cardew's attitude, Maclean sensed collusion between him and someone else to place Heredia in the East End Hospital. Cardew had lied.

If Maclean had witnessed Cardew's behaviour just after he quit the surgery, he would have been certain of his part in the plot to murder Heredia. Cardew first checked that his part-time secretary was typing his correspondence and medical records for that morning before shutting the surgery door and dialling a number. He said softly, "That Spaniard I was called to by your friend in the hotel – why didn't you tell me he was dead? I've just had one of his friends here checking on him and his wife – No, I didn't tell him anything, but you might have warned me ... You'd better tell the hotel woman to keep her mouth shut. I hope it doesn't mean trouble." Cardew replaced the instrument, gently; he removed and polished his thick spectacles. He crossed to the medicine cabinet to open it and produce a bottle of Scotch and a graduated beaker. A precise man, he poured himself exactly forty millilitres of neat liquor, gulped it down like medicine, carefully rinsed the beaker and replaced it with the bottle, imprinting both with the sweat from his nervous palm.

FOUR

A week later, when Deirdre and Maclean arrived at the

East London magistrates' court for the coroner's hearing about a dozen people had gathered in the foyer. Philip Rothwell came over to shake hands; he looked almost as disorientated as when the psychiatrist had stopped his drugs. "It's all cut and dried," he whispered. "I'm guilty." Maclean put an arm round him. "Nobody's guilty when he and a few other people know he's innocent," he said. Most of the others had come to give evidence, though Maclean spotted two members of the hospital management committee, obviously there to observe, take note of and act on the verdict. Scanning the assembly he saw no sign of Heredia's daughter or anything resembling her mother. A few minutes before nine o'clock, Pearson pushed through the crowd and beckoned them both outside. "'Fraid I've got nothing for you," he grunted. "Those prints you took have been through three different computers and each time they've come out as they went in. Not a smell of this man Heredia."

"What about Interpol?"

"Madrid's done its nut. Seems Heredia and his wife and daughter lived in a modest flat on the Avenida de la Libertad in San Sebastian. The daughter's here studying law at London University. Not a single entry on the police files, not even careless driving or spitting in the street."

"Yet, he looked as though he'd been in a bad accident," Maclean said. "Wouldn't they have had a record of that?"

Pearson shrugged. "Depends where and when he was hit who got the blame and if there was a police case afterwards. But I'll get them to check the files again."

"What did he do for a living?"

"He was an export agent for several firms making toys and figurines – bullfighting heroes and flamenco dancers, that sort of thing."

"An inconspicuous man with no secrets," Maclean murmured.

"And nobody to mourn him," Deirdre put in. When the court doors opened it seemed neither the wife nor daughter had appeared, nor anybody else representing the dead man.

They followed the crowd into the juvenile court-room where they were holding the inquest; all twelve jurors had already taken their places and a few minutes later the gaunt, cadaverous shape of Dr Geoffrey Y. Thurgood had taken its place on the bench and the coroner's officer had called the first witness. As Maclean listened to Thurgood's preamble and questions to Dr Hopkins, the pathologist, he realized the hearing was going to develop into an indictment of Philip Rothwell.

Dr Hopkins confirmed that death had been caused by cerebral anoxia, this oxygen depletion provoking respiratory and heart failure. "The anoxia was produced by a saturation dose of nitrous oxide and the effects of this were potentiated by a recent administration of Pentothal anaesthesia and premedication drugs." On and on droned the pathologist, describing the physiological consequences of such an error. Questioned by Dr Thurgood and woman juror about the amount of gas and the time required to starve the brain cells of oxygen, he replied, "About five minutes if the nitrous oxide were given in mistake for the oxygen dose and was therefore used in its most concentrated form."

"Is this what happened in your view?" the coroner asked, and Dr Hopkins nodded.

When he took the stand, Philip Rothwell did little to help his case. Nervous and hesitant, he left Thurgood, the jury and the audience with the impression of someone who could easily have mistaken one gas for another and misread the monitors on his anaesthetic trolley.

"Did you notice the patient's falling blood pressure and his failing respiration?" Dr Thurgood queried.

"Of course," Rothwell came back. "At that point, I gave him more oxygen."

"But you must have been aware this was merely increasing his distress," Thurgood sniffed. "Are you sure you were giving him oxygen?"

"Absolutely sure."

"How did you check this?"

"I turned off the tap of the nitrous oxide cylinder and verified the oxygen cylinder was on the right side and was functioning properly."

"Yet the patient dies from oxygen starvation," Thurgood said, the bite in his tone making an impression on everyone in the courtroom.

Both the surgeons, Hugh Digby, the consultant, and Roger Linton, his registrar, told how they had attempted by closed-chest heart massage and adrenalin injections to resuscitate the patient; but by then he had sunk into too deep an anaesthetic coma for them to help him. Bob Monk, the engineer, testified the trolley, cylinders and other equipment were working perfectly when he examined them half an hour after the patient's death. Both cylinders had enough pressure and the right gases in them.

However, one curious fact did emerge, when the night nurse, Susan Mallet, told how she had given Heredia two injections an hour before they took him downstairs to the operating block. "You say these were pethidine and atropine," the coroner prompted. When the girl nodded, he asked, "Are you sure the patient had no morphine that night, for the pain?'

"I'm certain, sir," Miss Mallet said. "I was on duty all that night and every time I opened his door he was asleep."

"What's all that about?" Deirdre whispered to Maclean.

"They found traces of morphine in the bloodstream and several organs during the post-mortem," he replied. "Somebody must have given him a short of morphine after his premed." Listening to the night nurse's evidence, Maclean was recalling Rothwell's impression of Heredia's arriving in the operating theatre almost anaesthetized; Anne Maxton, sitting five yards away, also seemed intrigued by this piece of testimony, and Maclean recollected she had come on duty that morning just after the shift changed at eight o'clock. It would have been simple for her to fill a syringe with morphine, slip into that private room and inject it into a man already drowsy from his other premed drugs.

It took Thurgood no more than two hours to gather all the evidence he wanted; his summing-up lasted no more than ten minutes and pointed the jury towards a verdict of death by misadventure. When the jurors filed back with this form of words, the coroner fixed Rothwell with his gaze then said, "I cannot endorse that verdict without a rider about the part played in this unfortunate accident by the anaesthetist, Dr Philip Rothwell. In my view, he deserves more than just a reprimand from the hospital authorities, who should overhaul their anaesthetic procedures to ensure no such deaths occur again."

Everyone filed out. Maclean was waiting in the foyer as Anne Maxton left the courtroom; she had a triumphant smile on her face, though her mood changed abruptly when she caught sight of him.

They said goodbye to Pearson at the door then drove Rothwell back to the East End Hospital. Knowing how neurotic the anaesthetist could be, Maclean cautioned him against doing or saying anything to anyone in the hospital, except to deny his guilt. "Whatever you do, don't resign. Let them fire you, and when we prove it wasn't your fault, they'll not only have to reinstate you but pay you handsome compensation into the bargain."

Rothwell was turning away when Deirdre called him. "Philip, we're giving a small party for Greg's tenth anniversary in Harley Street and we'd like you to come along if you can make it – wouldn't we, Greg?"

"Sorry, I forgot to ask you, Philip," Maclean said after a nudge from Deirdre. "It's just a private do. Can you come?"

Rothwell hesitated for a moment, then nodded. "I'd like to," he muttered.

"Seven-thirty," Deirdre said.

They watched him go to his car and drive off before Maclean turned to Deirdre. "What's all this about a tenth anniversary party? We've only been in Harley Street seven years."

"Seven years, three months and two days," Deirdre answered. "But since every day's the length of a wet Sunday, it seems more like twenty than ten years."

Maclean knew better than tangle with Deirdre's Irish logic. He grinned at her. "Who's coming to this private wingding?" he asked. 'And what's at the back of your Hibernian mind?"

"It's to cheer Philip up and stop him going back to that grim flat of his and getting drunk," Deirdre said. "I'll invite Joe Sainsbury and Jean and a couple of nurses from Harley Street." She tossed her red head

and shot him one of her more disdainful glances and
he knew what was coming. "You may be the
psychiatrists' psychiatrist but sometimes I think you
don't know much about human nature."

"It's true, mavournin," he admitted. "It's true."

FIVE

Carolina Heredia read the inquest report that
afternoon, slipping out of her Chelsea hotel to buy an
evening paper. Back in her room, she scanned the
article. They had swallowed everything whole – the
name Heredia, the explanations of the various
witnesses and experts, the thesis of medical negligence.
No one had probed beyond the operating theatre or
asked anything like the right questions. That young
anaesthetist had become the scapegoat. Now, if she
cared to enlighten the authorities about what she
knew …

She had hidden in this small hotel for more than a
week – since the day her daughter, Maria, had
telephoned with the news that Matthew was dead.
Immediately, she had thrown her belongings into a
suitcase, paid her bill and quit the Gatehouse Hotel on
foot. She neither liked nor trusted that trollop of a
hotel-keeper who had offered to ring a mini-cab.
Taxi-drivers could take you anywhere. Carolina
Heredia felt bewildered and frightened; she had just
lost the man she loved and was alone in a country she
had not seen for over twenty years, in a city that had

changed beyond recognition. Like herself. She carried a Spanish passport but had blond hair; she spoke native English, though with a slight Spanish lisp. Maria had scared her, implying Matthew's death was no surgical accident. He, himself, had whispered that he might not survive, in which case she and Maria should make for San Sebastian. If they need money, they could sell his confession. Roberts, the man she had met in Spain once, would pay good money for it. So would other people he had named.

At Queensway, she bought a tube ticket to Victoria where she deposited her baggage. Before taking any decisions, she had something she must do – see Matthew for the last time. She took a cab to the hospital, where she completed the formalities, then went to the morgue to offer a prayer for her husband. Even there she had a fright when that portly man had accosted her, offering help. How did she know he wasn't one of the men out of Matthew's past? She had run. When she returned to Victoria to gather her belongings, she had not the vaguest idea where to go. Her aged mother lived at Wimbledon, but she did not dare go there. Matthew's friends might know that address and keep watch on the house. She had a sister, Daphne, who was married with three children and lived at Chiswick; but she might endanger the whole family by seeking refuge there.

Finally, she alighted at Sloane Square. Off Kings Road, she discovered a small, private hotel called Eros House and booked a room for three nights. That night, she rang Maria and had a whispered conversation in Spanish. "Don't speak to anybody, don't eat in restaurants and don't go near any of your relatives," Maria exhorted. "And don't leave your passport or any papers lying around your room."

Carolina listened mutely, feeling hunted. She
bought her evening meal in a delicatessen, setting out
the cold meat and salad and slice of apple-cake on the
small table and eating it slowly with a bottle of
supermarket wine; she asked the desk to sent up a pot
of coffee and she laced the weak, bitter mixture with
some whisky. This revived her will. Unlocking her
suitcases, she began to sort through the clothing and
articles they had brought for the trip. His confession
lay under his sports jacket with his pocket-book,
passport, cheque-book and other papers.

She gazed at his Spanish passport with its grim
identity picture. Funny, they had both erased their past
so thoroughly, she had almost forgotten what his other
face looked like. One memory remained vivid – that
moment in the Hampshire house when they had
removed his bandages and she had observed his
bruised and battered and patched face. A different
man! "Still love me, ducks?" he had croaked. He had
five more operations to endure and it had taken her
several months to get used to the results. However, in
some strange way, she preferred his new face, scarred
and twisted as it was. It belonged to her, not to that
unbending virago of a wife he had fled. It was hers,
since Matthew had sacrificed his own features for her.
He had also stolen for her.

Why had they come back? After more than twenty
years abroad she would never have consented to return
but for one thing: his old mother had gone blind and
entered a home in Pinner; she had implored him to
make just one visit to her before she died. Of course,
Carolina knew their fortune had shrunk and she
guessed that Matthew had tried to twist the arms of the
men who had covered up his crime and his flight, and
benefited from both. Had he not fallen ill and nearly

died in that seedy hotel, they would have been on their way home by now. Carolina dried her tears. She picked up the confession on twelve sheets of foolscap paper in his bold, back-sloping hand, wondering for a moment what to do with it. Only this copy existed. Matthew had wanted it that way, saying if anything happened to him, she alone must decide what to do with it – sell it to his accomplices, hand it to the police, or burn it. Carolina felt that, from her viewpoint and Maria's, she had better destroy it and forget the whole story. Even if Matthew had been murdered, what could she do? Fighting a long battle to prove it would not bring him back.

However, Maria disagreed. When they met for half an hour at a small café in South Kensington, the girl suddenly asked, "Do you remember the two men you said you met in Spain – the ones who fixed my father's disappearance?"

"I only met one, a man called Roberts who knew your father well, and that probably wasn't his real name. And I only caught a glimpse of the surgeon who operated on his face, here in Britain."

"What were they like?"

Carolina thought for a moment. "I don't remember much about either of them. It's so long ago. And your father never wanted me to have much to do with these people."

"Because he didn't trust them," Maria said. "And he was right." She lit a cigarette and ordered another coffee for them. "That's why he wrote the confession," she said. "What have you done with it?"

"I was going to burn it."

Maria banged her coffee cup into her saucer. "*Madre*, you must not do that. They'd get away with everything, those men who murdered my father. All the names are there and you have the only copy."

"Your father wanted it like that," Carolina said. "And all I would like to do is forget everything and go back home."

"But will they let you forget it, those men? They will always be scared you're going to blackmail them, and if they murdered once they can do it again."

"What should I do?" Carolina asked, miserably.

Maria thought for a moment. "The police here are not like the police in Spain," she said. "With that paper, they would be forced to make a real investigation of my father's death and find the truth."

"But the scandal ..."

"*Madre*, you're worrying about our good name when we could be killed tomorrow. Go back and get it and telephone to Scotland Yard and give it to them and they will protect us until after the cremation and they will eventually arrest the murderers." Maria drained her coffee cup and rose, whispering that they should leave separately.

Carolina did nothing for twenty-four hours from the following day, a minor accident decided her him at the the police. She was walking back to her hotel, ft there. shopping, and had put up her umbrella against the drizzle. Half-way across a Chelsea street, she heard the rasp of tyres on the wet surface and a car skidded to a halt no more than six inches from her. After what Maria had said that event confirmed how someone could easily follow her in a car, wait his opportunity and stage a hit-and-run accident. Now a deep fear and suspicion infected her whole body giving everyone and everything a sinister appearance. She spent hours gazing at the street to reassure herself no one had her and the hotel under surveillance.

Next day, in mid-afternoon, she called Scotland

Yard from the hotel. She identified herself to a sergeant in the information room, explaining she had evidence that her husband might have been murdered. She gave the sergeant her address and phone number and he asked her to stay by the phone. There were certain formalities, he said. Three-quarters of an hour later, he rang back. Would Madame Heredia be good enough to remain where she was and do nothing? Someone at Scotland Yard wished to see her in connection with her husband's death. They would send an inspector with a car to pick her up.

She sat there for another hour, wondering what was delaying the police. Finally, the receptionist rang to announce a visitor and a few minutes later a slim man of average height knocked on her door; he introduced himself as Detective-inspector Brian Russell. First, he glanced at her Spanish passport and driving licence, then he quizzed her about her mother, her sister, her daughter. He wished to know Maria's address and she ＿＿＿＿＿＿ 'he whereabouts of her flat. He said, "'Fraid ＿＿＿＿＿＿ ask you to accompany me to the Yard,

＿＿＿＿＿ you take the information here?"

Inspector Russell shook his head. "Sorry, madam, but it might be a bit dangerous for you to be left on your own. Anyway, there are certain formalities requiring your presence at headquarters." He shrugged his shoulders. "It's not my case, but I know there are questions about the manner of your husband's death. We now have reason to suspect he was murdered."

"Suspect!" Carolina cried. "I'm sure of it." She stopped when the inspector put a finger to his lips and indicated the door.

"We'll talk about all that later," he whispered. Glancing round the room, his blue eyes fastened on the suitcases. He had a handsome face, what she saw of it between the trilby hat he wore well down on his forehead and the scarf knotted under his chin and tucked into his overcoat. He did not act much like a police inspector, though perhaps she had preconceptions about the police, whom she and Matthew had always shunned for their own good reasons and who, in Spain, emphasized their authority with revolver and truncheon. "Is that all you have to pack?" he inquired, pointing to the cases.

"Do I have to bring my things?"

"Perhaps they didn't explain that from now on you're under police protection," Inspector Russell replied. "Is that all you have?" he insisted.

"That and one or two toilet things in the bathroom."

"I'll help you get them together."

"No need," she replied, and began to fold and pack her dresses and other clothing. Russell embarrassed her by standing watching every move and gestu expecting her to bolt. As she came back bathroom with her toilet bag, she spotted table, leafing through some papers she had le He turned with a startled, almost guilty expression. She gathered up the papers and thrust them into a case. Her packing done, he helped her into her coat then preceded her downstairs and waited while she settled her bill. He opened the back door of his black sedan and installed her there, placing the cases in the boot. As he drove off, he obviously felt he could talk more freely. "You've given us quite a lot of trouble, Madam Heredia," he said. "We've been searching for you since you left the Gatehouse Hotel in Notting Hill. We just missed you there – you've quite a knack for vanishing." Turning, he grinned at her, then asked suddenly, "Why didn't you get in touch with us sooner?"

"I was afraid."

"Afraid of what?" he asked. "As I said, I'm not on the case."

"I was afraid of the men who murdered my husband, Miguel Heredia. He died during an operation in the East End Hospital. His real name was Whittaker, Matthew Whittaker." Somehow, it eased the burden of guilt on her to tell him this.

"Doesn't mean a thing to me, madam," Inspector Russell murmured. He swivelled his head and gave her a hard look. "Sure you're feeling all right?"

"I'm all right, and what I say is true."

"These people who're trying to kill you? Any idea who they are?"

"The same people who murdered my husband. He made a confession and wrote all their names down in case anything happened to him."

"And you have this confession?" His tone had a professional edge to it.

"It's in one of my cases," she admitted.

For several minutes he drove in silence, navigating through the back streets into Cromwell Road and crossing this to make for Kensington High Street. As they waited at traffic lights, he said over his shoulder, "You've nothing else that might help with our inquiries?"

"I don't think so."

"Your daughter – does she have any evidence?"

Something in the way he put these questions triggered her suspicions. For a detective who insisted he knew nothing about the case, he seemed well informed about her and Maria. Her gaze crossed his in the rear mirror; she noticed his curious blue eyes had

narrowed and his mouth had an ominous clench. At
that moment, in the raw afternoon light, she spotted a
strawberry-red birthmark on his cheekbone, below the
left temple. Now that she had seen before, for it looked
like a ragged sombrero. But where? Spain, just over
twenty years ago when this man had come out from
England to see Matthew. Carolina was almost certain,
even though this man had changed his appearance. He
was no detective called Russell but the man who went
under the name of Roberts, the man who had fixed
Matthew's disappearance. His disguise had fooled her.
She noticed those hypnotic blue eyes on hers and
dragged her gaze away from the birthmark; her spine
had turned to water and her legs felt weak and she
passed a hand over her forehead. "Anything wrong,
Madam Heredia?" the man asked.

"No, nothing," she got out.

Just before Kensington High Street, he swung the
big car right, then left into a tree-lined road bordered
with luxury villas. As she was trying to memorize the
street name, Grantham Villas, Inspector Russell
suddenly spun the steering-wheel left and aimed the
car into a ramp leading to a basement garage.
Everything from that moment caught Carolina
unprepared; she saw the garage door pivot upwards
automatically, then heard it clang shut behind them;
but then the bogus inspector had braked violently
shooting her forward, over the front seat and against
the dashboard, shocking and winding her. Before she
could recover, he had gripped her hair with his left
hand brought her head up and banged it against the
dashboard; with his other hand he had already
unzipped an airtight bag in the door pocket and from
this he pulled a swab of cotton wool and gauze. Despite
the woman's frenzied attempts to drag his hand away,

despite her scratching and struggling and kicking, he clamped the ether-soaked gauze over her nose and mouth and held it there until she was forced to gulp air and fill her lungs with the anaesthetic. Gradually her resistance ceased. For a moment, he studied the slack face with its closed eyes; he gave a deep sigh, then pressed a button to open the car windows and drew in several breaths free from the heavy, cloying tang of ether. When his head had cleared he searched the woman's handbag, cursing his disappointment that there were no papers on Heredia; he found two phone numbers on an envelope which he pocketed and a bunch of keys.

Carolina Heredia still lay unconscious. From his airtight bag, the man produced a long strip of surgical tape which he stuck firmly over the woman's mouth; her nostrils he plugged with damp cotton wool, clamping them shut with a surgical clamp. He sat there calmly, watching her face turn livid from oxygen starvation, his fingers on her weakening pulse. When the pulse had ceased he waited for several minutes before gently easing the tape away from her mouth which now sagged open. He cleared the nostrils. Nobody will ever think of looking for ether in her blood, he told himself as he carried the limp body to the rear of the car and placed it in the boot. Collecting her suitcases, he humped them up the stairs leading directly into the hallway of the villa. In his study, he emptied them of their contents and soon found what he was seeking – the confession written in a hand he knew well, Whittaker's. He put a match to the thick wad of paper, threw it into the open hearth and watched it being consumed. He closed the cases and carried them back to the garage.

Back in his study, he dropped two aspirins into a glass of water, watched them dissolve and swallowed the mixture. He drew the curtains and lay down, thinking that he had several hours to wait until nightfall and he could risk transporting the body to the river as near the woman's hotel as possible. Within a few minutes, he had fallen asleep.

SIX

Just before six o'clock, the phone roused Deirdre and she went to shake Maclean. "It's John Pearson," she said, pushing the receiver into his groping hand, then switching on the bedside lamp and placing a notepad and ballpoint pen on the table. "Sorry to break into your sleep, Dr Mac," Pearson said. "Know the woman you met in the morgue, the one you were trying to trace? I think they've just found her on the Thames bank – dead." Briefly, the detective gave what details he possessed and the address of the street nearest the riverbank where the body had washed up. "I'd like you to have a look if you can make it," he said. "I'm on my way." After the first few words, Deirdre had replaced the extension and pulled on slacks, a pullover and shoes. She had their car at the door by the time Maclean had dressed and come down. Even at that hour in light traffic, Deirdre took no chances in their tiny Fiat and it was nearly seven by the time they reached Tooley Street; they parked the car behind three police cars and walked through to the Thames. Pearson was waiting for them and led them down steps to the river edge and they squelched behind him through gluey mud up to their ankles. Deirdre's nostrils curled at the fetid odour issuing from the Thames mud; to compound her misery a drizzling rain started to fall out of the dirty clouds that shrouded London Bridge, Tower Bridge and the Tower of London the other side of the river.

A group of policemen were working round the body, making notes and taking pictures. Pearson whispered that it had been left there by the receding tide that morning and the police surgeon reckoned that Carolina Heredia had spent two days in the water. At a signal from the big detective, one of the local policemen pulled back the plastic sheet covering the dead woman and Maclean stared at a shrunken version of the face he had encountered in the morgue ten days before. She still wore the same jacket, though the river had ripped away her skirt, torn her silk slip and left her without a shoe and one of her stockings. On the tarpaulin beside her lay what her pockets had contained – a Spanish passport and driving licence, an identity card bearing her name, Carolina Juanita Heredia and an address in San Sebastian, also a card with her blood group. Pearson examined each item. "No sign of a handbag or any indication of where she was living in London?" he queried and one of the local detectives shook his head.

Maclean watched this routine reflecting that it looked like a simple suicide to those who knew nothing about this woman or her husband. But for his fleeting confrontation with the dead woman and his own inquiries, he might have agreed. When the local police learned that Carolina Heredia had lost her husband ten days ago, they would opt for suicide and close the file. He waited until Pearson, Deirdre and himself were alone with the body before examining it. Like Pearson, he noted the charm bracelet on her right wrist had a British hallmark, that her jacket and shoe both had Spanish labels. But it was her face that intrigued him; her eyelids seemed more discoloured than the rest of the body; he bent over to peer at them in the wan light, then studied the nostrils and lips. "That skin irritation could be caused by something like ether or chloroform," he murmured to Pearson.

"So, somebody did her in before throwing her into the river."

"Looks that way," Maclean conceded. "Somebody clever. Somebody with a bit of medical knowledge."

Maclean pointed out that the body did not have the waterlogged appearance of someone who had drowned herself and spent two days in the river and this also tended to prove she was dead before going into the river.

"We treat it like a murder, then," Pearson suggested.

Maclean glanced towards the two local detectives and raised a cautionary finger. "I'd keep this one to yourself and as few people at the Yard as you can," he said.

"But if it's murder …"

"You'll have a better chance of catching the man who arranged the murder of Heredia and his wife if you leave him thinking he has fooled you. And you might stop him from killing again straight away."

"Killing who – Heredia's daughter?"

Maclean nodded, then explained his reasoning. Whoever killed Carolina Heredia obviously did not realize anyone suspected that Heredia had been murdered and that crime camouflaged as medical negligence; so, he felt free to strike again, this time to dispose of another person who knew Heredia's secret and the identity of the murderer; like themselves, he would now be hunting for Señorita Maria Heredia to get rid of the third person who might incriminate him; and this killer might even imagine he could flush the girl out of hiding when she learned of her mother's suicide. Heredia's daughter evidently realized the danger, for no one had seen her since her father died, not even at the inquest. Maclean looked at Pearson. "Do you think you can fix it with one of your Fleet Street pals to run a couple of paragraphs calling this a suicide and publish that passport picture? You can ask for next of kin to contact Scotland Yard."

"Can do," Pearson said.

When everyone had finished and the body had gone to the morgue, the trio walked to an early-morning coffee bar on the Bermondsey Road where they ordered coffee and rolls. Within a few hours Pearson said that they'd have a fair idea of the time of death, if the woman had suffered bruises before her death, where she had been immediately before being dumped in the river and whether she had put up any resistance. He'd have a check made on hotels in the Inner London area and at the Spanish Embassy in case they knew anything. "Funny, she looks nothing like a Spaniard," he commented.

"Heredia only looked like one because he'd dyed his hair and wore those tinted contact lenses," Deirdre put in.

"They seem to have covered their tracks well," Pearson said.

"That's why I'm almost certain Heredia committed some crime – and probably in this country," Maclean murmured. "I'll give you ten to one he's on your files somewhere."

"But we've checked everything, even the prints you pinched, and come up with nothing."

"Say the man on that morgue slab was already technically or statistically dead – did you check that possibility?"

"I don't follow." Pearson swigged at his coffee and screwed his cigarette stub into an ashtray with a huge thumb. "At the Yard we only shove criminals into our 'morgue' file when we're sure they belong to characters who're really dead and there wouldn't be much percentage in keeping them in our 'live' file."

"But if Heredia's somebody else and he's either fooled you into putting him in your 'dead' file or bribed somebody in your Criminal Records Office into switching the prints or destroying them …"

Pearson grinned, then shook his head. "He'd be a clever rogue to do that," he said. "Nobody I've ever heard of has ever worked the substitution trick perfectly. There's always something left of a body to identify it. And if there's nothing left how can anybody prove they're dead?"

"That's the sort of Irish logic only Deidre understands," Maclean came back with a grin. "Just for my peace of mind, give Heredia's prints another go – this time through your morgue file."

"It'll cost you." Pearson passed a grubby pound note across the table to Deirdre. "You're the stakeholder – your boss owes me ten like that if he's wrong."

Deidre held out a hand and Maclean looked askance at it and her. "Ten pounds," she said.

"I don't handle money," he said, loftily. "Take it out of the office kitty."

"That's our rent and housekeeping money, what's left of it," she replied, still holding out her hand. "I didn't make the bet."

"But John's going to lose that," Maclean said, tendering his hand for the pound note.

Deirdre stuffed it into her handbag quickly. She looked at Pearson, who was grinning at this joust. "He'd make you believe all these stories about Scotsmen," she said. "When I squeeze parking-meter pennies out of him they're warm and smooth from the friction in his pockets. And when he goes to buy something in Portobello Road market, he dresses like a tramp so they'll pity him."

"Defamation," Maclean said, blandly.

"I'll honour his word and his bet," Deirdre said to Pearson.

When Pearson had gone, Deirdre reminded Maclean pointedly that he was a working psychiatrist and not a criminologist; he had a morning list of three patients at Harley Street and several others to see at the hospital that afternoon. She hurried him back to their flat to spruce up and get to his consulting-rooms to greet the first patient. When Maclean saw her his spirits sagged, though he bore up bravely, taking cover behind a dimmed light and, apart from some banal asides, allowing Mrs Woodruffe to recline on his couch with closed eyes and recite her monologue which she now knew like the Lord's Prayer. Algernon, her wicked husband, had been at it again – gambling away her fortune on slow horses, bad cards and the roulette wheels of a dozen London clubs; worse still, he was lavishing her money and presents on every painted whore and prostitute in the West End, filling their town flat with these abominable creatures and his boozing cronies. Doctor, if she could only stand up to him … If she had enough courage to try to live without him … If she could even venture into her own social circle without perceiving erstwhile friends whispering behind their hands about her, poor thing … If only she were

prettier, more seductive ... If only she had complete
control over her emotions ...

Maclean felt his own control slipping. One of his
regulars, Mrs Algernon Woodruffe heaved herself on
to his couch twice or three times a week several months
of the year to have her ego restructured and her
inferiority feelings buffered down to livable propor-
tions; for an hour Maclean listened, prompted,
encouraged, sympathized, conscious that he was
probably saving her from drink or drugs or quack
doctors. Money seemed the only thing the poor lady
had going for her; in her teens, her mother, a society
beauty had upstaged her daughter on every social
occasion, even rebuking her for her unprepossessing
looks; her sister, who had inherited her mother's face,
figure and high-handed ways, married a title and land;
and she, the younger sister, had fallen in her desperate
late twenties for a rake called Algernon Houston
Woodruffe, failed army officer, hammered stockbroker
and down-at-heel gentleman who had eyes only for her
money.

Poor Mrs Woodruffe! Maclean should really tell her
to take a stone off her waist and hips, have that
incipient dewlap massaged away, grab herself a young
playmate and spend some of her money on him and
herself. That would do more than a thousand hours of
free association or confession on his couch to fix her
ego and bring Woodruffe to heel. Of course, she had
that nose which repelled the hardiest of lovers. Even in
the penumbral consulting-room light, its profile was
traced starkly; it began with a deep cleft between the
eyes then started out fine until it reached the bridge
where it made a sudden, dogleg kink towards the tip
which itself had a slight twist. As Cyrano de Bergerac
and every practical psychiatrist knew, the nose by its

shape and olfactory action played a dominant role in human sexual behaviour. But with a schnozzle like hers, Mrs Woodruffe would only attract a younger Algernon with worse results. So, Maclean kept his counsel and tried to stifle his own guilt feelings about taking the lady's money. However, as Deidre argued insistently, Mrs Woodruffe not only paid half their rent, she allowed him to treat those needy cases that often spilled over from the East End Hospital and spend time on problems like Philip Rothwell which had little to do with his practice. Had he dared, he would have chucked this high-born lady and all the other well-heeled hostesses and socialites off his list. Mrs Woodruffe sighed. "Ah, Dr Maclean, if I only had my mother's confidence and elegance and my sister's beauty ..." she said, as though catching some distant echo of his thoughts. Privately, he considered her desire and ambitions beyond even the most brilliant combination of psychiatry and plastic surgery; however, he spent a good hour massaging her ego and sending her out to face another three days of social purgatory which she would doubtless recount next time.

Deirdre kept him slogging for another three long hours, filtering successively into his consulting-room a kleptomaniac youth who had graduated from shop-lifting through cheque frauds to car-stealing, a more interesting middle-aged woman suffering from hysteria, who had at least three distinct personalities and projected herself into several fantasy worlds, and finally a man in his fifties who had become impotent after a bout of nervous depression. Only when her clock struck one did Deirdre release them both for lunch. As they came out, she hissed at him to keep cave for traffic wardens while she fed the meter at which her little Fiat sat, the hunted look of a double-murderer on her pretty Irish face. She grimaced at the £60,000 of port-wine Rolls Royce occupying a whole parking-bay and almost elbowing her tiny car out of its space.

"Newcombe's, isn't it?" Maclean said, pointing to the elegant registration plate with the letters RRN 1 for Robert Randal Newcombe.

"It is that," she snapped. "And he ought to pay half my parking fee."

They walked to the small restaurant in Wigmore Street where Maclean ordered them omelettes with a mixed salad and a wedge of Roquefort cheese; Deirdre allowed him one glass of wine which he could take or leave, depending on whether he wanted to put his alcoholism cure to the test. He sipped the wine slowly, savouring its bouquet.

"Deidre, mavournin, long, long ago in your probationer nursing days didn't you see quite a lot of Anne Maxton?" he asked.

"No, not much of that one. She always thought herself a cut above the rest of us, so she didn't live in the nurse's wing at Guy's. Which suited everybody else."

"She wasn't very popular?"

"Popular!" Deirdre laughed so much she nearly choked on her lettuce leaf. "She was as popular as a smallpox case. She really thought she was something special because she worked with Sir Andrew Grant's firm in surgery …"

"You mean the great plastic surgeon? Who did the burned airmen during the war, and half the distaff side of Debrett's Peerage after it?"

"Not forgetting the film stars."

"So, she worked for him."

"Until his theatre sister kicked her out."

"What did they have against her?" Maclean asked. "Just her bossy ways, or the fact she was pretty."

"Pretty!" Deirdre had to take a long pull from her wineglass to swallow the word. "What makes you think she was pretty?"

"From what I saw of her, she was pretty."

"Well, I didn't look very hard at the inquest, but when I knew her she didn't catch many boy-friends." Deirdre stabbed with her fork at her jawbone, under the right-hand corner of her mouth. "She had one of those hairy moles just there, bigger than a rasp. And her eyes."

"Her eyes?"

"They were snake's eyes – green like that stuff that forms on copper."

"Verdigris?"

She nodded. "And her nose."

"Her nose?"

"It had a kink and a tip on it." Deirdre grinned. "As though it was dripping and the wind had changed and it stayed that way."

"Because she was naughty," Maclean suggested.

"In olden days, she'd have been roasted at the stake for brewing potions of human blood, bat entrails and snake venom."

"A witch?"

"A witch," Deirdre repeated.

Maclean was recalling what Rothwell had said about Sister Maxton; his own mild affair with her had turned sour, but according to him she had slept round the hospital. Maclean never believed gossip, yet he wondered who among her boy-friends had wrought the physical transformation in Sister Anne Maxton. "Was she especially friendly with any of the doctors or surgeons?" he asked.

"More than friendly with quite a few of them. And with her face, she had to make the running. Why?"

"When I saw her, she didn't have the mole or the drip on her nose," Maclean said, smiling. "I merely wondered which surgeon might have fixed her face. Did Sir Andrew Grant have any young assistants?"

"A good half-dozen, but most of them were just bag-carriers or spare hands."

"Remind me when we get in tomorrow to find out who toted Sir Andrew's bag in those far-off days."

Deirdre gazed at him. "You don't really think Anne Maxton had anything to do with the Heredia deaths, do you?"

"Not with the mother's death – but I wouldn't be surprised if she knows a bit about Heredia's death on the table."

Deirdre suddenly shivered and her hand trembled so violently that she had to put her glass down to prevent her spilling her wine. "What's up, mavournin?"

"I was just thinking, I wouldn't like to be in the daughter's shoes. She must be dead scared."

"What would you do if you were a foreign girl and thought somebody was looking for you to murder you?"

"Run for the nearest airport and home."

"But if she's too frightened and she's got nobody to go home to now, and she thinks they might follow her …"

"I'd buy myself some hair dye or a wig and some specs and different clothes and …" Deirdre thought for a moment. "If I got desperate I'd go to the nearest Catholic church and ask the priest for help."

Maclean grinned. For Deirdre with her Irish Papist background, the church and its ministers acted like lightning conductors, deflecting every almighty thunderbolt from god or devil.

When they parted company, Deirdre to return and type and edit his case-notes and tapes and he, in a cab, to the East End Hospital, all these questions niggled at him. He juggled mentally with the names of all the protagonists in the puzzle, injecting them into his mind one by one. Heredia, his wife and daughter, Rothwell, Maxton, the surgeons and the nurses at the operation. Going through the main hall of the hospital, he stopped at the kiosk to buy an evening paper. Pearson had good contacts for Señora Heredia's picture stared at him from the front page with a caption relating her suicide after her husband's unfortunate death. What would that story stir up? As he went up in the lift he hoped his brain would yield some small lead or clue or some inspired deduction. And quickly. For the man who had arranged Herendia's death and had murdered his widow was looking for the third member of the family, Maria Heredia.

SEVEN

Maria Heredia had tried, vainly, several times to contact her mother at the Chelsea hotel, but from the receptionist she learned Mrs Black had booked out of her room three days ago. At first, the girl imagined that she was following advice and moving every week to elude pursuit; yet she had not taken the hotel room Maria had prospected for her in Old Brompton Road. Now the girl decided she must call at the hotel, find out what had happened and if her mother had left a message or a phone number. She had got as far as Victoria in the tube when a man entered with a morning paper and took a seat beside her. When he opened the paper, Maria glanced idly at it and went rigid with fright at the sight of her mother's passport picture. At the next station, Sloane Square, she ran upstairs to buy a paper then ducked across the square, through hooting cars, into a snack bar. She bought a cup of tea and sat down to read the caption. Suddenly, she felt sick and had to rise and run to the toilet where she vomited into the handbasin. In the mirror, her face seemed shrunk, drained of blood. Fear knotted her stomach again and she retched for several moments though nothing came up. She splashed water on her face and let her hands run under the tap until she thought herself strong enough to walk out of the café. On the pavement outside, she stood, oblivious of the faces crowding past her. It was false. Her mother had never killed herself. Not when she had finally intended to place her father's confession before the police and request them to seek the murderer. It seemed her father's killer had got to her first. But how? She must make her own investigation, though prudently. If they had trapped her mother, they might still be watching the hotel, waiting for her! Again, she glanced at the story. It related that her mother had been in the Thames for two days. That frightened her even more. She had passed on her girl-friend's phone number. Had her mother written it down? If whoever murdered her had found that number and traced the flat where she was staying, her own life would not count for much. Maria entered the post-office in the square and rang her girl-friend, telling her to pack her few belongings and leave them with the porter at the university law faculty.

Maria had the impulse to flee, to get out of London, out of Britain. But she quashed that notion. Any remaining doubts about her father's murder had disappeared now they had murdered her mother. If she ran where would she go and when would she stop running and how would she ever square cowardly flight with her conscience?

She knew her mother's hotel, less than five minutes' walk away. However, it took all her courage and will to venture along King's Road and up the narrow street to the Eros Hotel. Behind a desk off the lounge sat a middle-aged man in a waistcoat and shirt sleeves with silver hair. Maria asked if Mrs Black were in her room. He scrutinized her over his half-moon spectacles. "Haven't you read the paper?" he asked, thrusting his copy at her with her mother's photograph showing.

Maria looked. "Her name was Heredia — I didn't know," she stammered.

"We've had the police here asking about her," he said.

"When did she leave the hotel?"

His forehead puckered. "Three days ago, it was. She phoned and somebody came and picked her up."

"Who was he?"

He shrugged. "Just said he was a friend and Mrs Black was expecting him."

"Did she leave anything in her room — two suitcases?"

"No, she took the lot, paid her bill and left with her friend in his car."

"What was he like, this man?"

At this question he peered searchingly at her then wagged a finger. "Sorry, miss, if you want more information, go and ask the police. I've told them everything I know."

Maria thanked him and left the hotel. Go and ask the police! Her mother had probably done that, and finished in the Thames. And in that newspaper, Scotland Yard had the effrontery to request next of kin to claim the body. She wandered back to Kings Road, deliberating where to stay that night. Her own Kensington flat would be watched, like her girl-friend's flat in Bloomsbury; and with no other friends, she would have to find a private room or stay in a hotel. Her thoughts orbited round one question: how had they managed to trap both her parents so easily? To her knowledge, her father had made only one visit, to his aged mother in her clinic at Pinner; her mother had not even dared to meet either her mother or sister. Maria could only think, like her mother, that her father had secretly contacted his old accomplices and they had followed him to his hotel and bribed that witch of a proprietress and that effete doctor. So, she must not commit the error of contacting anybody who might give her away.

A siren bellowed behind her and an ambulance cut its way through the thick traffic. Gazing after it, Maria had a sudden idea. Who was the other casualty in this whole business? Rothwell, the young anaesthetist she had met at the hospital. They had reprimanded and sacked him. Maria made for Chelsea public library where a librarian traced him in the medical directory and register. His flat in Holland Park Avenue was listed in the phone book. From a callbox, she dialled the number but it did not answer. Maria took a bus to Notting Hill and walked through homegoing crowds down the broad, tree-lined avenue to the old house where Rothwell had his flat. His bell did not answer so she tried the ground-floor flat. A middle-aged woman with a ghoulish face came to the street door. "Try the pubs," she croaked when Maria asked about Rothwell.

On the north pavement there were half a dozen pubs and Maria inspected them all before exploring those on the network of streets leading off the avenue. On the point of giving up, she pushed into a tiny pub in a side-street and spotted Rothwell sitting, head-down, in a corner. From ten yards away, she could tell he was drunk. When she approached and stood before him, he stared dully at her neither recognizing her nor remembering he had treated her to coffee in the hospital refectory before her father's operation. "I'm Maria Heredia," she said, finally.

"What're you doing here?" he asked in a slurred whisper. "If you've come to put the boot in and accuse me of murdering your ol' man ..."

"I came to ask you for help," Maria said, interrupting him.

Rothwell flicked his eyes upwards at her. He gulped some of the liquor in his glass, then raised his head and laughed in her face. "Me help anybody! I can't even help myself."

Maria produced the newspaper she had folded to carry in her handbag; she thrust it at him, open at the inside page and at her mother's picture. "Haven't you read the paper?" she asked.

Rothwell gave a twitch of his head, signifying no. Fumbling in a pocket, he emerged with a crumpled cigarette which he lit with an unsteady hand. "After last week, I stopped reading papers," he said. "I didn't exactly get rave notices in Fleet Street for my role at the inquest."

"But I know you had nothing to do with my father's death," Maria exclaimed. She came round the table to sit on the lounge seat beside him. He gazed at her blond hair, then her serious face. "I remember how good-looking you were," he said.

"Never mind that." She placed the story in front of him. "Do you remember meeting my mother in hospital?"

Rothwell let his eyes travel slowly over the picture, then followed each printed line with his index finger as though he was having difficulty focusing. He turned that sluggish look on her. "So what?" he asked. "She did what I feel like doing – chucked herself in the drink."

At this callous indifference, Maria nearly got up and left; but she restrained herself, folded the paper and put it away; she then placed her mouth close to his ear and said, firmly, "My mother was murdered by the same people who killed my father."

Rothwell fixed his dull eyes on her once more. "And who are they, may I ask?"

"I don't know," she replied. "But we can find out."

"We!" Rothwell said with a slow grin, pointing at Maria then turning the finger on himself. Shaking his head, incredulously, he beckoned to the barman who approached. "Two whiskies," he said.

"I do not wish anything to drink," Maria said, but Rothwell waved aside her objections. Paying for the drinks, he handed her one glass then raised his own to her. "What you've said deserves a toast," he said, ironically. "Here's to We." To placate him, Maria took one sip of the strong liquor which rasped on her throat and set her coughing.

"If we find the murderer, it'll clear your name," she said.

He looked at her, his eyelids blinking slowly, then he drawled, "I've got no name left – and anyway, I'm not sure you haven't found the murderer."

She nearly yelled at him to stop feeling sorry for himself but bit her tongue and replied, calmly, "Don't you know they used you, the people who killed my father?"

"What's it matter now?" Rothwell gulped the last of his whisky and was trying to catch the barman's eye to order another when Maria tugged at his sleeve. "Dr Rothwell, please don't drink any more. Please." Something of her appeal penetrated his fuddled head. He let his hand collapse.

"Sorry about your parents," he muttered. "Come on." He rose, shakily, and knocked over a couple of chairs on his way to the door. Maria supported him with her arm. Outside, he turned to her. "Where do you have to go?" he said.

"I've nowhere to go," she replied. "I wondered …"

"I've got a sofa," he said.

Maria had never seen anything like his flat. His double bed still lay, unmade, from that and previous mornings; his clothes he had stepped out of and left on the floor, or thrown over chairs; papers and magazines were strewn over the living-room table and sofa and he had obviously left that day's dishes on the dining-table from lunchtime on a table-cloth that had not been changed for more than a week. Ashtrays heaped with cigarette butts sat everywhere and added their acrid tang to the stale air in the room. Rothwell waved a lax hand at the mess. "You can see I'm a bachelor," he said.

To keep her mind and hands occupied and prevent her from thinking, Maria washed up the dirty crockery and made a strong brew of instant coffee which she carried through to Rothwell, persuading him to drink it. He ventured into the kitchen to help locate some ham and eggs which she fried and set before them on the coffee-table with bread and butter.

"I've forgotten your name," he said when they had eaten.

"Maria – Maria Heredia."

Rothwell pointed to the bedroom. "Maria, you take the bed and I'll sleep on the sofa."

"No, I am making the bed for you," she said. "But do you not wish to hear about my parents?"

He shook his head and she could see he was dropping with weariness and the effect of drink. "Tomorrow – tell me tomorrow or I won't remember a thing about it," he mumbled.

While he went into the bathroom, Maria made the bed and tidied the bedroom. Rothwell grabbed a pillow off the bed and found two covers which he handed her, explaining where she would get a pair of clean sheets and a set of his pyjamas. Tossing his clothes one by one over a chair, he flopped into bed without pyjamas and within minutes had fallen asleep.

Maria arranged a bed on the sofa. In the bathroom, she had to rinse her mouth with water since she did not even possess a toothbrush. A medicine cabinet lay ajar and she noticed a bewildering array of bottles containing pills and potions. But it was the syringe and packet of disposable needles that caught her eye. She wondered if Rothwell suffered from diabetes. Closing the cabinet and putting out the flat lights, she climbed into the makeshift bed. Only in the darkness, when her mind had no other stimulus to occupy it, did she realize how alone she was. Her parents' faces flashed across her mind, as she had last seen them and as she remembered them over the years. Warm tears ran down her face and in a moment she was sobbing without restraint and continued to sob until she had no tears left. In the square behind, the church clock chimed the hours until three o'clock before she dropped into an exhausted sleep.

EIGHT

Maria woke next morning wondering where she was until her mind fitted together her memories of the previous evening. Rising, she tiptoed to the bedroom, puzzled to discover a rumpled and empty bed when the alarm clock said only seven forty-five. She went into the kitchen to make herself some coffee. An empty glass stood in the sink. It smelled of whisky. A key clicked in the flat door and Rothwell appeared embracing a paper bag which he deposited on the kitchen table. Out of it he produced milk, rolls, half a dozen eggs and butter, then a jar of marmalade. He eyed her up and down, smiling at the way she had turned up his pyjama legs and sleeves and tied her fair hair in a loose knot over the nape of her neck. "Now I remember you," he said. Making a gesture at his purchases, he said, "Your breakfast."

"I shall make you something."

"I normally have a hair of the hound that bit me the night before, some coffee and three aspirins." He lit a cigarette. "Anyway, I'm due at a gynaecology clinic to give gas an hour from now."

"Gas?"

"Anaesthetics. It was the only job I could get, part-time, when the hospital kicked me out."

"But if you are working you must eat breakfast," she insisted. She put on three eggs to boil and started making coffee and toast. He helped her set the table and within quarter of an hour they had sat down to eat.

"I remember you said something last night about your mother," Rothwell remarked.

Maria nodded. She ran to produce the newspaper from her handbag. He ran his blue eyes over the picture and caption, then looked at her. "It says suicide quite clearly – no foul play."

"She was murdered for the same reason as my father," she said. "Shall I tell you why?" Rothwell nodded assent and she continued. "My father was a man called Matthew Whittaker. He was English, like my mother."

"I wondered about a blue-eyed, blonde Spanish girl," he cut in.

"Just over twenty years ago, my father owned a firm near London for making pharmaceutical medicines. He got into difficulties and stole money, an important sum of money, from his firm. There is a word for it."

"Embezzling."

"That is the word," she said, nodding. "He faced imprisonment, so he decided to disappear and leave proof that he was dead."

"So that's why he had plastic surgery."

"He had help from several people – perhaps members of his firm and others," she said. "I do not know who they were, for my parents did not want to involve me. My mother followed my father abroad and I only know what she let drop over the years."

"So, you think the people who helped him disappear murdered him to prevent him giving them away, then murdered your mother, is that it?" When the girl nodded, Rothwell gazed at her. "You know what that means – you're in danger, too."

"I don't mind that," Maria said. "I am going to find

those people who killed my parents even if I have to do it alone.''

Rothwell lit them both cigarettes. "Why not hand this information over to the police and let them handle the investigation?"

"No." Maria shook her head emphatically. "That's what I told my mother to do, and she's dead."

"Did she contact the police?"

"I cannot be sure. She called somebody and was met by a man with a black car and nobody saw her again alive."

"But how can you hope to find the murderer?"

"I can start with my father's old associates," she replied. Then there is a surgeon who altered my father's features. He also knows something."

"I admire your courage," Rothwell said, then shook his head. "But even if you did flush out the murderer, do you think he'll admit it and allow you to hand him over to the authorities?" Rothwell drained his coffee cup, took a last mouthful of toast and marmalade, then rose. He checked his briefcase while she watched him.

"You're not going to help me?" she asked.

"I don't see how," he said. "If I were you I'd take what you know to the police." At the door, he paused for a minute. "If you haven't found anywhere to stay you're welcome to your bed." Returning to a small writing-bureau in the hall, he opened it and pulled out a set of keys. "Those are for the street door and the flat door," he said. "Put them back there if you go for good."

Maria accepted the keys and thanked him for his offer. When he had gone she tidied the flat, had a bath and dressed. After collecting her things from the porter's lodge at London University, she would find a room somewhere and perhaps follow Rothwell's advice and contact the police with the information she possessed. As she was finishing dressing the phone rang; for a moment she deliberated whether to answer it, then finally picked it up.

"Hallo, is Philip there?" a woman's voice asked.

"No, he has gone out one hour ago," Maria answered.

"Oh! Who am I speaking to?"

"I am a friend of Philip."

"Excuse me for asking, but you're not English, are you?"

"No, I am ..." Maria caught herself. "I am not English."

"Are you a student?"

"No," Maria lied.

"Do you know Philip well?"

"Tell me who you are and I can take any message for Philip," Maria said.

"Don't bother, I'll pop round and see him this evening," the woman said and Maria heard a click as she hung up. Somewhere Maria had heard that inquisitional voice before, though she could not place it. That call left her uneasy. Yet, she let herself out of the flat and walked along the avenue, scanning every newsagent's window, reading the notices to see if she could find a room to let. After noting several addresses she went by tube to Russell Square, walked through to London University and collected her suitcase and holdall from the porter. A cab brought her back to Holland Park and she humped the luggage upstairs into Rothwell's flat to leave it there while she inspected the rooms. First, she visited those in the area north of the avenue and found two, in Ladbroke Grove and Queensdale Road that might suit her; for lunch she ate an omelette in a small restaurant on the south side of

Notting Hill Gate and afterwards did some shopping to replenish Rothwell's larder, buying eggs, cold meat, vegetables and a stick loaf in a delicatessen. It had begun to drizzle when she started back for the flat and she hurried, head-down, through the throng, quickly opening the street door and entering the hall.

Everything happened so quickly that for a moment or two she felt too stunned to be shocked. Then she panicked. As she closed the door someone leapt at her, clamping one hand round her mouth and the other round her throat. In her terror, Maria dropped the plastic shopping-bag and tried to squirm free. But she felt that hand tighten round her windpipe, choking her and forcing her head back. In desperation, she drove her elbows backwards into his body, but his thick coat tamped the blows. Now her head was hammering with blood and bursting for lack of air. Forcing her mouth wide open, Maria bit with all her strength on the hand covering her nose and mouth. She heard the man yelp with pain and release his hand. In a minute, she had wrestled herself down under his other arm, freed herself and turned to run. But he caught her once more, this time spinning her round, gripping her neck with both hands and squeezing. His face was grimacing with the effort, his mouth contorted with hate. Even in that penumbral light, she noticed his startling blue eyes beneath the trilby hat. Maria was trying to scream, but not a sound came from her choked throat; she stamped on his feet and felt the eggs crunching on the lino beneath them both. She wriggled and wrenched at his hands but could do nothing to free herself from that grip. Her sight was blurring, her other senses were going. In a moment she would be dead if she did not act. In a last, despairing effort, she lashed out with her foot, striking his shin-bone. As he tensed with the pain, she brought her knee up under his coat and buried it in his crotch. He gave a grunt, then his breath exploded in her face. His hands dropped in a reflex action. Maria took a great gulp of air and ran for the stairs. Behind her, his feet were clattering and she could tell he was gaining on her. On the landing, she halting, knowing she had no chance of reaching Rothwell's door. Her assailant had come half-way up the stairs. Those strange eyes bored into her as he advanced, almost hypnotizing her. Maria waited until he had all but reached the landing. With both hands, she grasped the banister rail, then lunged out first with one foot then the other. She caught him on the shoulder, then on the face. As he toppled backwards, his hat rolled off and she glimpsed grizzling, light-brown hair receding at the temples before she turned and bolted up the remaining two flights of stairs, fumbling frantically for the flat key. It took an eternity finding the lock, opening the door and banging it behind her. Clipping the chain into place, she collapsed on the hard chair in the hall and shut her eyes. Her heart was pounding in her head and she was sick with fright. Where her attacker had grasped her round the throat it felt too raw to swallow.

All had gone quiet. When she had recovered her breath and her heart had steadied, Maria rose and went into the bathroom. Among the jumble of bottles, she unearthed a packet of soluble aspirin, dropped two tablets in a tumbler of water and gulped the mixture. Going to the window, she looked both ways along the pavement. No sign of the man who had attacked her – just ordinary people hurrying through the rain. How had he known where she was hiding? Maria lay down on the sofa and replayed in her head everything she had done since learning of her mother's death. She could swear no one had followed her around that morning and she had spotted no one suspicious when she collected and brought back her things. Had someone identified her in the pub last night and followed them home? Were they watching Rothwell? She suddenly recalled the prying voice of that woman who phoned. Had she recognized her Spanish accent and alerted the man who had just tried to kill her? He obviously knew where to find her. Rothwell might know who she was.

Maria dozed off and came to when somebody started banging on the door. It was dark. She rose and crept through the hall. "Who is it?" she said, fearfully.

"It's me – Philip."

Edging the door open on its chain, she verified he had no one with him then opened the door.

"What's all the cloak-and-dagger stuff?"

She could smell the drink on his breath and noted he swayed slightly. "Somebody tried to kill me," she whispered. "He attacked me at the foot of the stairs."

"So that's what old Ma Skinner was chuntering about. She's complaining like hell she'd a mess on the stairs."

Maria explained she had bought food and dropped it and did not have the courage to go back and clean up the mess. Rothwell stood listening while she recounted what had happened. "This woman, the one who phoned – what did she want?"

"She asked me all sort of questions – who I was, what I was doing. I think she might have guessed about me."

"No name?" She shook her head. "And the man who attacked you – sure he wasn't trying to rape you?" He shrugged. "It happens a lot around here."

"He was trying to strangle me," she insisted. "He may be the man who killed my mother."

"And he may not be," he said, sceptically. He conducted her into the living-room, switched on the light and studied the bruises on her neck. "Anyway, he's a sadistic bastard," he muttered.

"Dr Rothwell …"

"I'm Philip."

"What do I do? Where do I go?"

"Get out of here," he said. "Go back to Spain and do what your father did – change your name." He looked at her face and his washy-blue eyes crinkled into a smile. "A girl like you can do that no bother – a lot of men would tumble over each other to give you their names."

"I'm not running and I do not want to get married," she said. "I want to avenge my parents." She gazed at him reproachfully. "And if you stopped feeling so sorry for yourself and getting drunk every night you would help me and clear your own name." She pointed to her suitcase. "If I can stay tonight I'll move these tomorrow to one of the rooms I saw."

Rothwell nodded. Hanging up his coat and cap, he went to the drink cabinet to pull out a bottle of whisky some of which he sloshed into a glass with a little soda. He swallowed this greedily then poured himself another. He caught her staring at the glass and twirled it in his hand. "It helps me wind down and dissolves my problems," he said with a lop-sided grin.

She studied him for a minute. Despite the flippant manner he had a sad face and remote eyes for a man she estimated to be not yet thirty. "My father used to say that," she replied. "But drink doesn't solve any problems – it creates more problems."

"You talk like Dr Mac."

"Who's Dr Mac?"

"Gregor Maclean. A psychiatrist who knows all there is about drunks and junkies and **hopheads.** Probably because he was a drunk himself.''

"Then why do you not listen to him?''

"I should,'' Rothwell conceded. Then, as a paradoxical reflex action, he poured more Scotch into his glass. "Maclean saved my life not from one death but a thousand deaths.''

"What do you mean?''

"I was a junkie.'' Rothwell went into the bathroom to return with the syringe she had spotted. He held it up. "You know how people who've given up smoking keep one cigarette there to remind them how difficult it was and they're only one tobacco-filled paper tube away from addiction. Well, I keep an empty syringe there to stop me going too far with this'' – he jabbed a finger at his glass – "or with anything else, and getting hooked again.''

"How did you become – what is it? – anyway, a drug addict?''

"How?'' He conjured a cigarette from the packet in his hand. "Easiest thing in the world for a gasman like me. You sniff the anaesthetic gases to see you've got the right ones. They give you that lift and you want to go higher and higher and finally you land on cocaine, then heroin, and that's oblivion road, the loneliest road in the world. And if nobody turns you off it, you die the death of a thousand nightmares.'' Rothwell lit the cigarette and dragged the smoke deeply into his lungs. He looked at her. "If you want to know why I became a junkie, that's more difficult and you'd have to ask Dr Mac.''

Maria looked at her watch. It was seven-thirty. "There's nothing much to eat,'' she murmured. "I was too scared to do any more shopping.''

"All my tins finished then,'' he said with a wry grin. "I'll go and get my staple supper – fish and chips. That suit you?" Maria nodded, and he went on, "There's an Indian grocer open along Latimer Road and I'll stock up with bread, milk, eggs and one or two other things for tomorrow."

She helped him into his coat. "Don't be too long, Philip," she said. Rothwell nodded. He pulled down a switch on the intercom speaker in the hall. "I'll squawk into this when I'm at the front door," he said.

Maria put the heavy chain on the door and drew the living-room and bedroom curtains. Outside, the street looked fairly empty and she watched Rothwell until he turned the corner into the back streets, then went into the kitchen where she made fresh coffee and crisped what remained of their bread in the oven.

Ten minutes after Rothwell left, she heard a click through the intercom speaker. It crossed her mind that he had not wasted much time shopping and he had forgotten to announce himself. She strained her ears for his footfall on the wooden stairs but heard nothing. Yet, someone was inserting a key in the lock! Some sixth sense alerted her. Letting the kettle boil, she tiptoed from the kitchen through the hall. Fear tingled along her spine as she noticed the door edge open and a gloved hand come through to fumble with the chain. Maria gave a yell and rushed forward, throwing her shoulder and all her weight behind the door, jamming the gloved hand and bringing a moan of pain from the man on the other side. She saw the hand open abruptly and the fingers writhing before she was hurled backwards when the man thrust the door open until the chain held it. His hand disappeared. At that moment, the girl had the presence of mind to slam the door shut and snap home the safety-catch. Running to the phone, she dialled any number and shouted loudly enough for the intruder to hear, "Give me the police."

Footsteps rumbling and receding on the stairs told her he had fled. Switching off the flat lights, she parted the curtains and observed a shadowy figure emerge from the street door and scuttle along the avenue to the left. But where had Philip gone? As she stood there wondering if she should call the police she saw two men supporting a third who was pointing at their door. A minute later, she heard Philip's voice come weakly over the speaker. "Maria, it's me. Come down and let me in."

"No, Philip, listen. Ring the woman on the ground floor and she'll open the street door. And come up alone. I'll tell you why later."

Rothwell complied. When she let him in, he collapsed in a living-room chair. "Somebody mugged me," he gasped. "He must have followed me down Latimer Road. He pinched my wallet and key-ring."

"He wasn't interested in your money," Maria said. "He wanted the keys. If I hadn't put the chain on the door and I hadn't heard him over the loudspeaker, he would have got in." Fetching hot water, she cleaned the blood off his face and scalp where he had been hit. A wound about an inch long lay open in his scalp. As she worked, she explained what had happened. "It was the man who tried to murder me earlier today," she said.

"I'm beginning to believe you."

Maria finished swabbing the wound. "You need three or four stitches in that," she said. "Have you got a doctor."

Rothwell nodded and went to the phone, dialling a number. "Deirdre, is your boss there?" he asked. After a second or two, he went on, "Gregor, I've got somebody here you should meet. Can you come over now and bring a suture needle and some catgut? Oh, and ask Deirdre to fetch something tasty from your fridge for two hungry people."

NINE

Maclean shaved round the scalp wound and stitched it while Deirdre took over the kitchen and fried the two steaks she had brought, delegating the cooking of chips and beans to Maria. She listened while Deirdre chattered in her soft Irish brogue, telling her she could not longer stay here with Philip now that her parents' killer had traced her whereabouts. There was a mews flat – it belonged to a woman doctor on research fellowship – and she, Deirdre, had the key. They would not leave Maria on her own in the flat. Deirdre would come and share it with her until they had tracked the murderer.

Maclean and Deirdre kept her and Rothwell company while they ate. Maria was fascinated by the baggy, paunchy figure of the psychiatrist who spoke with a burring Scottish accent and cracked jokes against himself and his medical breed. Anyone meeting him casually might have lent credence to those stories that psychiatrists behaved more quaintly than their patients; yet he drew more information out of her in ten minutes than she knew she possessed.

When Deirdre mentioned her plan to share a flat with Maria and suggested Rothwell might move in with Maclean, the psychiatrist scoffed at her. "Miss Heredia doesn't need a duenna or a watchdog," he said. "And what would Philip and I do shacked up with each other. An ex-junkie and an ex-drunk – that would be a dynamite combination for you." He turned to Maria and stabbed a thick finger at Rothwell. "Do you trust him?" he asked. Maria nodded. "Then he shares the flat with you. Just see he doesn't empty too many Scotch bottles." Maclean looked at Rothwell. "And you, Philip – just let anybody get near enough Maria to harm her and I'll forget my oath and throttle you slowly with my bare hands."

When they had cleared the table, he prompted Maria and everyone listened while she recounted as much as she knew of her father's story. From her handbag, she produced pictures of her father, Matthew Burden Whittaker and his father, who had been a prominent London chartered accountant. When her father left grammar school he decided to study pharmacy for three years, although he had also inherited his father's flair for book-keeping and figures. First he gained sales and management experience with an international drug firm. At 26, he married a woman five years older who had enough money to set him up with a small firm that made indigestion tablets, cough remedies and other over-the-counter preparations; he also imported and sold medical instruments like stethoscopes, sphygmomanometers, syringes by direct mail order to the medical profession and hospitals. Her father was very shrewd in business. He spotted that several important patents on antibiotics and tranquillizers were expiring; he had some of those drugs manufactured abroad cheaply and undercut firms who had a sellers' market in the National Health Service in Britain. Through skilled advertizing in the medical press and direct-mail promotion, Matthew Whittaker boosted his sales and expanded his business to the point where Whittaker Pharmaceuticals employed two hundred people. But he spent as well as earned. In his middle thirties he fell in love with Maria's mother, Janice Grainger, who was fifteen years younger. By 1958, Whittaker was beginning to run into trouble; he had pirated patents that had not expired and lost two court cases costing him more than £100,000. His business, too, was losing its thrust. Around this period he began to plot his disappearance and was already planning a series of complicated frauds which Maria did not understand. Her mother had joined him six months after he vanished, working in Paris and Geneva as a secretary to cover her tracks before making for Spain. He had chosen that country because he already had a passport in the name of Miguel Contreras Heredia. Maria's mother said so many people had died or gone missing during the Spanish Civil War he could have chosen a million names. She, Maria, had been born on the Costa Brava. As a child, she had travelled everywhere with her parents, staying in the best hotels or rented villas on the Côte d'Azur or the Italian Riviera and even making trips to South America, Mexico and the United States. They had lived in San Sebastian for ten years where her father had set up a small import-export toy business that had accounts ledgers and a registered office, nothing more.

"Why did he come back and risk exposure?" Maclean asked.

"His mother is very old and thought she was dying and implored him to visit her before she died."

"Was that the only reason?"

Maria shrugged. "He told me no other."

"But he might have looked up some of his old friends to see if they could help him out for old times' sake."

Maria said she realized much of the money her father had invested had eroded through inflation, and the rest had gone on high living. Perhaps Dr Maclean was right and he had thought of blackmailing those people who helped him plan his disappearance and fake his death. She did not know for sure.

"Did he or your mother ever mention these accomplices?"

"No, never. My father wrote a confession with their names, but he made only one copy which he gave my mother for her alone to use at her discretion. She would have used it."

"And that's gone with her," Maclean said. "Did he ever mention the name of his plastic surgeon?"

"He did not," the girl said. "But my mother once said his operations lasted two months and were done in a private house somewhere in Hampshire. She had nightmares about that experience."

Maclean picked up the faded and dog-eared snaps of Whittaker and studied them. "His eyes seemed light here, but somebody said Señor Heredia's were brown," he remarked.

"My father always wore special contact lenses because his eyes were very sensitive to light," Maria said. "I saw him twice with them out. His eyes were blue, light blue."

Maclean did not quash the girl's illusions but handed back the snapshots. He had a last question. "Why do you think anyone would kill your father and your mother and then try to kill you because they had helped your father make his escape twenty-odd years ago? At the most, a court might sentence them to a few months' imprisonment for false pretences or aiding and abetting the crime of embezzlement."

"I have wondered myself," Maria replied.

Deirdre broke up the party, saying Maria looked tired and had endured enough for one day. She could sleep at the flat with them that night until the mews had been aired; in any case, Philip had to stay and change the locks on his door tomorrow before joining Maria. With the girl beside her and Maclean filling the back of the small Fiat with two bits of luggage, Deirdre drove them home; she helped Maria unpack and make her bed. When she came back into the living-room, Maclean was poring over his notes on the Whittaker case.

"Greg," she said. "Do you think it's wise to let Philip share a flat with that young girl?"

Maclean raised his head and looked surprised. Sometimes Deirdre allowed her Irish Catholic morals to get the better of her good sense and logic; she also overlooked the fact that she had been living in sin for years with someone who believed love a stronger bond than any marriage contract. So he said, tongue in cheek, "I know how you feel about Philip, macushla – but he's old enough to look after himself if Maria's Spanish ways get the better of her and she tries anything."

Deirdre lifted her eyes to the ceiling. "You know very well what I mean," she snapped. "It's the other way round."

"But she went and threw herself at him."

"Because she was scared."

"And needed help and security." Maclean took Deirdre's hand. "They're both orphans – she's just seen her parents killed and he never had any to speak of. Let them work things out." She only half-swallowed this and he perceived as she tidied the flat that she was still pondering how to resolve this moral dilemma. Sometimes he had to balk Deirdre's efforts, especially if they interfered with his own schemes like this one. Before she could come back with another attack he said, "Mavournin, I hope you haven't paid John Pearson that ten pounds."

Her russet head nodded. "Of course I did," she said.

"Well you'd better ask him for our money back. Heredia must be in their files – only under the name Whittaker."

"I can't do that," she cried. "A bet's a bet."

Maclean grimaced. "I suppose so," he said. He gazed at her serious face. "Tell you what – you'll have to reimburse me since you slipped up by paying him." He extended his hand. "It's eleven pounds, isn't it?"

Obediently and innocently, Deirdre went to her bag and solemnly counted out eleven pounds which Maclean pocketed. Deirdre went back to her routine tidying and washing up. Suddenly, she burst out of the kitchen and marched over to him. "You're a crook," she said. "You didn't put up a penny of that money. That was my money I paid John – ten pounds and his own pound."

"What does that mean? – I gave my word about paying the money if I lost," he replied, blandly. "And you made the mistake, mavournin, didn't you?"

Deidre stood there, speechless at the enormity of his confidence trick which had driven everything else out of her head, including her moral strictures about Rothwell and Maria.

TEN

Maclean not only tangled with Deidre and her morals but with John Pearson, who could not imagine any member of the Metropolitan police taking graft or aiding and abetting criminals. "But I tell you, John, the girl's mother is supposed to have phoned somebody in the Yard just before being collected by her murderer. For me that's too long a coincidence." Pearson still refused to believe they had a nark in police headquarters, even though he, himself, had checked with the Eros Hotel proprietor. He and the psychiatrist were sitting in a small café in St James's Street, a few steps from Scotland Yard, and Maclean had just outlined the gist of Maria Heredia's story.

"Are phone messages posted in the information room?" Maclean asked.

Pearson nodded. "But they're also circulated to the various department heads, even up to the Commissioner's office. Forty or fifty people see them minutes after they're logged."

Producing an ebony snuff-box and opening it one-handed, Maclean built a small mound on the back of his other hand and sniffed; he trumpeted into a polka-dot handkerchief. "Somehow we've got to peep at Whittaker's file without alerting anybody in the Yard," he remarked. "Where do you keep those records?"

"In the basement, if they're the 'dead' ones. The 'live' ones are microfilmed and on the computer."

"We want the dead ones."

"Mac, if I listen to you they'll hand me a truncheon and my old waterfront beat."

Yet he did listen, then signed Maclean through the security check in the front hall and led him down in the lift to the records section. Of the two, the big detective looked the more guilty as he showed his card and they passed into what they called The Morgue. There, they confirmed Matthew Burden Whittaker still existed – as a wad of paper and a small box of exhibits. "We can't take them out of here without a signature," Pearson whispered.

So they sat among the dust and mouldering paper under the fluorescent lighting and read through the Whittaker file and examined the pictures taken before his disappearance; they studied the blackened partial denture that had belonged to him, the Rolls razor, a wrist-watch, a ballpoint pen monogramed and a silver box for tablets; they split the file, reading in turns the Fraud Squad report on his embezzlement, the hunt for him, the discovery of his charred body in a London hotel gutted by fire and the coroner's inquest that had declared him officially dead.

"He got away with quarter of a million pounds," Pearson exclaimed. "Good money in those days."

"There must have been more to it than money," Maclean said. "Plastic surgery and all this" – he pointed to the box of exhibits. "He could have chosen a dozen countries where he'd have been safe from extradition for embezzlement, including Spain."

Whittaker had planned the theft and his escape meticulously, at least a year ahead. Then, he had opened accounts with three of the Big Five banks – a

private one and two for business. Since he moved half a
million pounds a year through these accounts, he
frequently went into the red, though never for much or
for long. His credit stood high and the three bank
managers considered him a friend as well as a good
risk. Whittaker then persuaded eight of his staff to
open accounts in their own names, but to let him
handle them. He paid them a small fee and swore that
those accounts would never be overdrawn; they would
serve to extend his credit, boost his business and
secure their jobs. Using cheques drawn on those
accounts as collateral, Whittaker began to increase his
borrowing, even raising money on the eight 'accommodation' accounts. It required a juggler's skill to
keep just the right money circulating through all those
accounts, but Whittaker never once ran a serious debit
balance on any of his proxy accounts before disappearing. And he timed his final operation perfectly,
persuading his friends, the three bank managers, to
advance him quarter of a million pounds in credit to
launch a new wonder drug that existed only on paper
and in his imagination. Two weeks later, when he had
planted the money in Switzerland, he vanished.

    Maclean and Pearson compared pictures of Whit-
taker and Heredia. No one would ever have taken
them for the same man. Whittaker's nose had been
flattened and its tip modified, his jut chin had been
given a cleft; with his facial patches, Heredia looked
like an accident case; and, to complete the disguise he
had darkened his blonde hair and wore tinted contact
lenses. "By the time your worldwide alert went out, this
was the man you were looking for," the psychiatrist
said, pointing to the Heredia pictures.

    "What!" Pearson scoffed. "A week after he
scarpers."

"No, his surgery might have taken a month or two – but before the Yard heard of his disappearance, Whittaker was in a private house with his face covered in bandages. And he emerged as Heredia."

"But how did he fool a Yard doctor and dental expert and land in the 'dead' file?" Pearson demanded. He pointed to the denture and X-ray pictures. "That denture is Whittaker's, and the skull records compare as well as the shoes, clothing and bits and pieces."

"Whittaker knew exactly the evidence that would convince the police and he got it all together before he vanished. Even down to the X-rays and his denture. Heredia had upper and lower false teeth."

"But he couldn't have planted these things himself," Pearson objected.

"No, I'd say he had several accomplices, one of them with access to police files."

"And of course they happened to be on hand when the Ladbrook Hotel went on fire two months after Whittaker's disappearance," Pearson said with heavy sarcasm.

"The Ladbrook or any other hotel," Maclean said. "There's a hotel fire in London every week in winter. Somebody had all those props ready to drop among charred bones." He pointed to the blackened objects in the exhibits box. "If your chemists had analysed the soot they'd have discovered it came from a coal fire or a wood fire."

When they emerged from the archives, Maclean offered the detective a meal at his flat so he would learn what Deirdre had done that day. When they entered, she slipped Maclean a small package and he disappeared into the bathroom for a few minutes, returning to pour Pearson a Scotch and himself a tonic water. Pearson was staring at him. "Mac, there's something wrong with you," he said. "It's your eyes – they've turned green."

Maclean lowered his large large head and, like some conjurer, removed the contact lenses from both eyes. Pearson observed that, apart from a small transparent space for the pupil, they were tinted green. Maclean had also palmed into his hand another set of lenses, slightly thicker but also coloured. "These were the original of the type Heredia was wearing," he said. Such lenses were designed to be implanted behind the cornea and tinted to treat albinism, the pigment deficiency which affected the iris of the eye and allowed too much light to pass. Only certain eye surgeons and perhaps a few plastic surgeons who used them aesthetically would have known about this new technique at the time Whittaker disappeared.

"We must find out who ordered those for Whittaker," Pearson said.

"We're working on it, John."

When they had eaten, Deirdre showed them her other research findings. She had seen Whittaker's dentist and discovered the company director could easily have procured his dental records; he had become very friendly with the dentist and his nurses, often drinking coffee with them in their office while waiting his turn in the chair. "And, of course the files were there and nobody would miss them while he had them copied," Deirdre said. She had also visited Fleet Street where the *Daily World* librarian, a friend of Maclean, had photocopied everything from their file on Matthew Burden Whittaker. As they looked through this bulky packet of cuttings, Pearson's eyebrows lifted in surprise. "They've got more stuff than we have in our police records," he commented.

"I wonder why," Maclean said with mordant irony.

Maclean selected the cuttings from the Ladbrook Hotel fire. "John, have a shufti at these Scotland Yard men who're investigating the fire and see if you recognize any of them."

Pearson spread out the half-tone prints, yellowing and friable, and peered at the four men in the basement room with the powerful magnifying glass the psychiatrist handed him. "That's Detective-inspector Bernard Carpenter," he muttered, aiming the glass at one of the men. "He was in charge at Notting Hill Gate and one of the best. The others I wouldn't know. Before my time." However, he picked up a couple of the cuttings. "I'll see if I can get anybody at the Yard to identify the other three," he said.

"Just watch who you approach, John."

When Pearson had departed, Maclean donned an outsize apron with London scenes on it that wobbled and oscillated with the movements of his paunch, and helped Deirdre with the washing-up. "I didn't tell you, when I got back to the consulting-room, Mrs Woodruffe ambushed me," Deirdre said. "Algy's off on one of his betting and sex binges and she's had another eating binge. She went through ten of my paper hankies."

"That's just a small helping of what I suffer twice a week – for your sake."

Deirdre sent several dishes bouncing precariously into the washing-up machine. "For my sake!" she exclaimed, rising to the bait.

"Well, you say keep her on the books because she pays half our Harley Street rent."

"Know what she wants now? – a nose-bob, if you please." She threw him a probing look, then murmured, "Now I was after wondering who injected that thought into the lady's neurotic head, and suggested I should arrange the operation."

Maclean's forehead puckered. "Come to think, I did once mention that according to Freud and certain post-Freudians, the nose has great sexual significance."

Deirdre tossed the dish-cloth at him in her anger. "And did you also happen to mention that the best nose-bobber in the business is Mr Robert Randal Newcombe?" Her face was flushing as red as her hair. "That – that – that crook."

Maclean put an arm round her shoulder, but she wriggled free of his grasp. "Now, now, mavournin," he wheedled. "Don't forget Newcombe and I are both in the same trade. I fix their psyches and he repairs their egos. I make it possible for them to face the world and themselves and he makes it possible for them to stand the sight of themselves in their dressing-table mirrors."

"And charges them five hundred pounds or a thousand for his half-hour's work while we toil for months on patients for a pittance."

"It's small change for Mrs Woodruffe."

"All right, you fix her operation," Deirdre retorted. She slammed the remaining dishes into their slots, banged the lid down and started the washing-up machine. She thumbed at the saucepans and other utensils, signifying that he could finish on his own, and stalked out of the kitchen. Maclean realized her ire would soon evaporate, for she had not threatened to catch the next Irish boat or Aer Lingus plane and lose herself in the mists of Ireland.

ELEVEN

In mid-afternoon, Philip Rothwell locked his flat, emptied his postbox, picked up his Metro and drove to Bayswater. Remembering Maclean's injunctions, he chose a roundabout way through back streets, halting at road junctions to check that nobody was tailing him. Since they might have registered his car number he parked half a mile from Nelson Mews and humped his suitcase to the flat. Maria opened the door on the security chain, then let him in. It looked a typical mews flat in a row once belongings to the façade of Victorian mansions behind them and used to house coachmen and stable their horses. Its stable had become a garage and upstairs had been transformed into a luxury flat with four rooms on the first floor and a run of wooden stairs into two large rooms giving on to a flat-roof terrace.

Maria explained that Deirdre had installed her that morning early. "The flat has everything," she breathed, showing him the fitted kitchen with split-level cookers, teak bench, cork floor and every type of automatic gadget. Each bedroom had its bathroom, one with a sunken bath. "Choose," she urged but seemed so crestfallen when he pointed at the sunken bath that he changed his mind, and they both laughed. "It's the sort of house I've always dreamed about," Maria said. "In a kitchen like this I can make the best paella Valenciana you have ever tasted with chicken, lobster, prawns, mussels, everything. You can have suckling pig and Spanish fritters and ..."

"Hold on! Where'll I find all that stuff?"

"I've already bought most of it for several days."

He stared at her. "But Mac ordered you to keep off the streets and let me do the shopping."

"You went shopping last time," she said, accusingly. "Anyway, Deirdre was with me and we kept off the main streets." She looked at him, a question in her eyes, then uttered it. "Deirdre and Dr Maclean are not married and yet she is a Catholic."

"Don't ask me why," Rothwell said. "It's got something to do with the fact that Mac was driving with a skinful of drink, he had a crash and his wife died. That turned him into a real drunk and Deirdre weaned him off the bottle the hard way."

"The hard way?"

"She was his nurse at an alcoholics clinic where they dried him out. It was her job to feed him whisky and inject a substance called apomorphine which made him vomit up the whisky. She kept him on that in a closed room until Mac couldn't look at a whisky label without being sick. It's called aversion therapy, but it's a form of torture. When he left the clinic, Deirdre came with him."

Maria was listening with a rapt look on her face. "Now I know why they love each other and depend on each other – even if he teases her. They do not need a marriage contract."

Rothwell nodded. "I suppose Deirdre warned you about me."

"She said you were too fond of girls and drank too much – but she also explained about you."

"My home truths," he said, wryly. A smile crinkled

his mouth. "Tell her I didn't touch a drop of drink last night and I'm taking my chaperonning duties seriously."

Rothwell studied the street-door and window-shutter locks. They had patent locks and bars embedded in the floor and walls. Maria held up the four keys Deirdre had given her, handing him two. "They're both for the front door." She rapped on the dining-table, two short knocks three times with a long pause in between. "You knock like that if you forget your keys – and please do not lose them this time."

"Maria," he said. "I'm sorry about yesterday – I mean doubting what you said."

She shook her head. "I'm the one who is sorry for making them attack you." Making him remove the cap he wore, she looked at his injury. "How does it feel?"

"I was hit where it hurt least," he said, shrugging.

To while away the time, they played Scrabble, then watched a film on TV before Maria went to prepare her famous paella. Rothwell watched her, appraising her lissom figure and slender, shapely legs; he wondered what her face really looked like without either the wistful or frightened expression that had never left it since they met. Having heard her story and part of her parents' story, knowing the ordeal she had gone through, he marvelled that she had retained her calm quality of innocence. Deirdre was right to warn her about him. However tempted to seduce her, he must remember this scared and lonely girl trusted him.

"Philip," she said as she was setting the dining-table, "you look very serious."

Rothwell shook his head. "I was just thinking I'd be glad when Mac and the Yard man nail this man who attacked you."

"Are you so anxious to get rid of me, then?" she

asked, gazing at him, sadly.

"Well," he grinned. "Let's say I don't like the responsibility of holding your life in my hands." How could he tell her he was going to find her too pretty by half to share a flat with?

TWELVE

Deirdre drove along the alley of lime trees, past the sweep of evergreen shrubs and rhododendrons to the clinic, a former manor house on the edge of a golf course between Harrow and Pinner. Wedged tightly into the front seat of the miniature Fiat, Maclean was studying the well-barbered lawns and gardens and wondering who paid for Whittaker's mother in such a luxury twilight home. A nurse led them along gleaming, antiseptic corridors to a small common-room on the second floor, overlooking a pond and the ninth green. Mrs Whittaker sat in a corner, her back to the French windows, her face immobile and half-hidden by dark glasses; her massive body had sagged and spread at the waist and thighs to overlap the seat and arms of the wheelchair in which she rested. She was babbling to herself, long word sequences uncoiling from her blue lips in an unbroken torrent. Taking the old lady's hand, the nursed called into her ear, "This is Dr Maclean, who's come to see you, Mrs Whittaker." She nodded, though without interrupting her mono-logue. For several minutes, Maclean and Deirdre sat listening to this mental playback of Mrs Whittaker's daily routine in the Ealing flat where she had spent most of her life; she chit-chatted with her cat, the daily woman and the welfare worker as if they were before her dead eyes; she recounted what she heard on her radio and recalled phone conversations; she detailed her daily meals and even mumbled knitting patterns. Finally, Maclean broke into this maundering soliloquy.

"Did Matthew, your son, ever phone you?" he called into the hand he cupped over her ear.

"Matthew's dead these twenty years," the old woman said, then lapsed once more into her chuntering recital as though turning her blind eyes inward to describe scenes from her hermetic life as they flickered across her mind.

"The police are now certain he didn't die," Maclean called. "They know he faked his death and he's been living in Spain for twenty years." At this, the unseeing blue eyes blinked and seemed to glitter strangely in the spring sunlight; for a moment, the monologue snapped shut before continuing. Maclean gave Deirdre an apologetic shrug then whispered, "I'm afraid I've got to shock her out of herself." Taking the old lady's hand, he said, "You knew Matthew was here, in Britain. He phoned you two weeks ago, didn't he? — just before he came to see you."

"No, it's not true," Mrs Whittaker said, the words bursting from her lips.

"Did nobody come to tell you Matthew died ten days ago on the operating table?"

That silenced her. Deirdre shook her fist at him as they saw tears coursing from the old woman's eyes. More poignant, she began to jabber about her son, how good he had been to her as a boy and man, how clever and generous he was. "He only came back to see me," she mumbled.

"Did he see you?"

"Yes." She shook her head. "But I could not see him."

"Just as well for her," Deirdre hissed at Maclean and he nodded. What would this woman, with her total recall of things, have made of the transformation in her son's face? Her blindness had spared her that shock.

"And Janice," Maclean said. "Did Janice see you or phone you?"

"She came with Matthew and she phoned when he went into hospital – that's all. Is she all right?"

"Yes, she's all right," Deirdre lied.

As though she wanted to unburden herself, Mrs Whittaker told how her son had sent her money every quarter through her bank; how, a year after his disappearance he had begun to write to her through an accommodation address.

"You mean he used a third person," Maclean prompted. "Who was it?"

"It was Margaret," the old lady sighed. She was relaxing into her interior monologue again when Maclean shouted in her ear, "Margaret who?"

"She was his secretary – the girl I thought he should have married – she wanted so smuch to marry him ..."

"Margaret who?"

"Margaret – Margaret – Cowley, I think. Oh, dear, my memory's gone – she's married anyway – I don't know her married name."

"Margaret received the letters and phoned you at home with what your son wrote, was that it?" Mrs Whittaker nodded slowly. "And she took down what you wanted to say in reply and wrote to your son at another accommodation address?" Again, she nodded.

"Where did Margaret work?" Deirdre asked.

"With Matthew at his firm – such a pretty girl – dark hair like a crow's wing and beautiful hands and such pretty dresses – she'd come with her car and run me into the country and we'd lunch and sit for hours – I can see the trees turning yellow that last time we stopped at Chalfont St Giles and had tea with muffins and honey – you know in that shop there …"

Maclean tried, vainly, to cut through this stream of talk with more questions about the old lady's relationship with Margaret; but now in full flood, Mrs Whittaker had blocked off everything that threatened to penetrate her personal narrative. They both shouted their thanks in her ear then retraced their way through the sprawling manor-house to their car.

"What do you make of all that?" Maclean asked as they drove through the grounds.

"At least we know this Margaret was another person who realized Whittaker wasn't dead – beside the plastic surgeon, the accomplices and possibly Maxton."

And Margaret took care to keep in touch with the old girl, knowing she'd be the first to hear if her son attempted to return."

"But if Whittaker spurned her for another woman, she must be in the plot with other members of his firm," Deirdre said.

"We can find out tomorrow," Maclean said. "John Pearson has fixed a meeting at Whittaker's old factory to have a chat with the directors who worked with him."

"Tomorrow's too late," Deirdre objected. "By then they'll have found out from Margaret that we've seen the old lady. And if the murderer's among them, he'll know we know about Whittaker."

"You're right," Maclean said. He looked at his watch and saw it was coming up to midday. "We can catch

John before he leaves the Yard and get him to ring
them and say we'll be along this afternoon."

THIRTEEN

John Pearson joined them for lunch in a small
restaurant off the High Street, near Harrow School. To
give their visit to Whittaker's old factory an official
stamp, he had brought a police car. During their meal,
he told them what he had gleaned about the company
from a Fraud Squad man who had looked at the books
after the scandal. "With what he pinched and the debts
he'd run up for the firm, Whittaker left them more
than half a million pounds in the red," he said. "A lot
of cash to find."

"And yet they didn't go bankrupt," Deirdre
remarked.

Both looked at Maclean, but he merely shrugged
and said to Pearson, "You'll have to ask them why,
John." He had his own private notions about
Whittaker's plot and the firm he had run, but he did
not want to reveal too much to the Yard man. For two
reasons: Pearson might start flashing search-warrants
at Whittaker's old associates, going through their
books, opening their bank accounts and generally
scaring them off; secondly, he still had a niggling
suspicion about that phone call Maria Heredia's
mother had probably made to Scotland Yard invoking
help and bringing a murderer to her hotel room. A less
honest policeman than Pearson would have connected

that call and its consequences, the fact that the Yard files on Whittaker were surprisingly light and other factors pointing to a corrupt colleague.

Pearson drove them to the factory Whittaker had founded in West Ealing in the early fifties. It had changed its name to New Biomedics and now had a yearly turnover of two million pounds and profits of two hundred thousand pounds. It had three directors: Ronald Forster Cripps, chairman and managing director, Dr Michael Seddon Barnes, medical director, and George Armstrong Wrigley, company secretary. At first glimpse, New Biomedics was doing handsomely. It lay between Western Avenue and Greenford Road in an old private estate and used the original mansion as its administration building. Grafted to this structure was a modern two-storey, chrome-and-concrete factory and laboratory. A secretary led them to an office in the mansion where three men greeted them. Pointedly, the detective produced his police card; he introduced Maclean and Deirdre by merely saying they had a semi-official involvement in the case. Ronald Cripps introduced himself then his medical director and company secretary. "Did I understand you to say on the phone it had something to do with Matt Whittaker, our late, lamented chairman?" Cripps murmured. "We all knew him well."

John Pearson had produced his notebook and was studying it with all three directors eyeing him closely. Maclean scrutinized them. Cripps looked immaculate from the trim of his greying hair through his Savile Row suit, silk shirt and tie with gold pin and cuff-links down to his manicured nails and his exclusive cigarettes. His office, too, reflected this elegance, furnished in genuine Chippendale with Impressionist art on its panelled walls. He must bomb the room with aerosol disinfectant behind Wrigley, Maclean thought, for the company secretary had dandruff like snowflakes on his cheap suit, a face as grey as rain, and scrawny, yellow fingers with dirty nails. Barnes was a dapper, precise figure of medium height. His brown eyes darted like a ferret's behind rimless bifocals; he had a cleft chin and thin, bloodless lips.

"This is a routine inquiry, gentlemen," Pearson said, lifting his head from his notebook. "I'll put the questions to Mr Cripps, but if you other gentlemen have anything to say, you can do so." He pointed at the tape-machine and intercom apparatus on the desk. "Are these things switched on?" Cripps shook his head and shot a perplexed look at the others. Maclean gave the detective full marks; he had set the formal tone and made the three directors wonder. "How well did you know Matthew Burden Whittaker, sir?"

"We all knew him very well indeed," Cripps said. "I worked with him for five years up to his disappearance and death," he continued. "And Dr Barnes knew him before that."

"I knew him about eight years," Barnes put in. His voice had a high-pitched, metallic ring.

"So, you really believed the story that he died," Pearson said.

"Of course he died," Cripps exclaimed. "Everybody knew that. Story! What do you mean, story?" If Cripps was lying, he lied as he did everything, impeccably.

"I have a surprise for you," Pearson said. "But you must keep this between yourselves. Whittaker did not die twenty years ago. He died just over a fortnight ago."

Cripps's greenish-blue eyes widened and he arched his head back in astonishment. He produced a gold cigarette case, extracted a tipped cigarette and lit it.

"But they identified his body a month or two after he vanished. He died in a hotel fire, didn't he?"

"Yes, they had medical evidence to prove it," Barnes interjected.

Pearson shook his head. "That was to convince the police," he said. "Matthew Whittaker staged his death. We know exactly how, though I can't disclose this to you. However, I can tell you he was living abroad all this time under an assumed name with false papers and he came home to visit his aged mother."

"How did he die?" Barnes asked.

"He died on the operating table of a London hospital during surgery for a stomach ulcer." Pearson paused, then said, solemnly, "Do I have your word that you knew nothing of this?"

"Nothing at all, Inspector – nothing at all," Cripps replied. "I'm absolutely flabbergasted." Barnes and Wrigley both nodded their concurrence with his remarks.

Pearson thumbed over another page of his notebook. "We know that Whittaker must have had one or more accomplices to plan his disappearance and fake his death. Did he at any time approach any of you to help him?"

They shook their heads, then Barnes asked, "How did he prove to you he was dead?"

"That I cannot tell you," Pearson said. "Did any of you know he had extensive plastic surgery on his face?" Again, they shook their heads looking for all the world to Deirdre like the three wise monkeys who never saw, heard or spoke any evil. "We're trying to trace the surgeon who performed these operations," the detective went on. He broached the subject of the embezzlement and they all denied any knowledge of Whittaker's theft until after he had gone. "How did you succeed in keeping the company in business when he left you with debts of more than half a million pounds?" Pearson asked.

Cripps managed a wintry smile. "It was pretty hard going. We had to sell the buildings and the ground to meet most of the debts, then raise enough capital through the banks to start a small firm manufacturing basic drugs."

Pearson filled half a page of his notebook with this information, then gazed at each of the directors in turn. "Can we come to the present?" he said. "Whittaker might have looked up some of his old friends when he returned. I must put this question to you – did he approach any of you for financial help?"

"Certainly not, Inspector," Cripps said, and the others nodded. "We would be the last people he'd come to knowing how we all felt about his behaviour and not one of us would have concealed the fact that he was still alive, let alone assist him."

Pearson produced a copy of the *Daily Express* from his coat pocket and Maclean watched the three men stare at it, puzzled. "Did any of you know the woman who followed Whittaker abroad – a Miss Janice Grainger?"

"There was a girl called Grainger who worked in the firm for a short while," Barnes said. "Matt was friendly with her. Was that the one?"

Pearson nodded. He opened the paper at the picture of Whittaker's companion, then passed it round the three directors. "None of you noticed that she committed suicide just over a week after her husband's death."

Cripps looked at his partners and shrugged. "Sorry, Inspector," he murmured. "I probably looked at the picture, but people change in twenty years and the name Heredia didn't suggest anybody that I or the others would know."

Maclean and Deirdre had merely listened to the dialogue between Pearson and the directors, and the psychiatrist waited until the Yard man had closed his notebook before speaking. "Would you mind if we had a look round your factory while we're here?"

Cripps hesitated for a moment, then shrugged at the other two directors. "Not at all," he said. "I'll act as your guide myself." He led the way across a steel bridge joining the manor-house to the second floor of the factory, a modular arrangement of laboratories and small production units. In one section, a team of men and women were making and bottling liquid antacids and anti-spasmodic preparations; in another corner, a machine was stamping and packaging tablets of the same medicine other small groups were tending robot equipment producing spansules to treat the common cold and allergic conditions like rhinitis.

Maclean noticed that in each of these labs and workshops up to half a dozen closed-circuit TV cameras were monitoring the staff and their operations. He had no doubt that Barnes and Wrigley were sitting in the control room tracking their progress with their spying system. Cripps was explaining they had similar units on other floors to make certain hormones, cortisone and antibiotic preparations; his firm also acted as British agents for some European companies, manufacturing their drugs on licence. He was marching quickly across one factory area when Maclean stopped them. He picked up a bottle of white, crystalline powder from a shelf and gestured at the various chemicals on the workbenches.

"I see you make LSD," he said, holding up the bottle of lysergic acid."

Cripps inclined his head. "We make just a little for experimental purposes. It goes to psychiatric hospitals."

Maclean replaced the half-litre flask. Sold on the black market that potent drug would have fetched a good hundred thousand pounds and sent a few thousand addicts on fantasy 'trips'. In adjoining labs and workshops in the same section small teams were making amphetamines, the powerful mental stimulants, and barbiturates. Glancing at one of the TV cameras, Maclean said, casually, "I suppose you have to watch theft with these drugs."

"Theft!" Cripps repeated with a note of surprise. "All our staff are handpicked and vetted carefully. We have automatic control on every ounce of chemical we handle. And for good measure we spot-check the staff going out every night."

He was leading them past the showroom at the factory entrance hall when Maclean pulled them up once more. "What sort of medical equipment do you do?" he asked indicating the ranks of syringes, manometers, sphygmomanometers, proctoscopes, ophthalmoscopes.

"Mostly imported stuff," Cripps murmured.

Pointing to the various oxygen masks, Maclean said, "I suppose you supply oxygen bottles as well, do you?" Cripps nodded. "And nitrous oxide?" Cripps threw him a curious glance before replying.

"We have a few dental and hospital clients since Whittaker's time," he said, curtly.

Maclean and Deirdre exchanged glances. Matthew Whittaker had died because somebody tampered with the cylinders of oxygen and nitrous oxide, substituting one for the other. But did the bottles with the wrong markings come from this factory? They walked to the police car and as he opened his door, Maclean turned to Cripps saying almost as an afterthought, "By the way, did you have someone called Margaret Cowley working for you during Whittaker's time?

"Cowley? Cowley?" For several minutes Cripps tried the name on his memory. "What did she do?"

"His secretary, I think."

Cripps flashed his teeth. "Matt was a bit of a ladies' man and he changed his secretary as often as his blotter. Cowley?" Finally, he shook his head. "I don't remember that one, so she couldn't have lasted long."

As they drove back, Pearson turned to the psychiatrist. "Well, what do you make of Messrs Cripps, Barnes and Wrigley?" he asked.

"Cripps would make a hit with the Royal Shakespeare Company. He talked too much and the others too little. But I'm sure those three men knew Whittaker was coming back to see his old mother – and possibly to put the screw on them. And this woman, Margaret Cowley, that nobody remembers probably tipped them off."

"Did you see all that oxygen and laughing-gas equipment?" Deirdre said.

"They had the motive and the means," Maclean murmured.

FOURTEEN

Immediately the squad car disappeared, Cripps loped upstairs to his office where Barnes and Wrigley were waiting for him. Cripps checked the door was locked and the intercom off before opening a drawer and playing back the tape he had secretly recorded. Twice, all three listened to the dialogue before Cripps spoke.

"Who's this man Maclean?" he asked.

"He's a pal of Rothwell, the anaesthetist blamed by the coroner for Whittaker's death," Barnes said. "He's a Harley Street psychiatrist.

"A head-shrinker," Cripps muttered, contemptuously.

"Yes, but he's different."

"Have you met one that wasn't?"

"I mean he's clever and cunning behind that fat face," Barnes went on. "He appeared at the Archer murder trial and several others as a defence witness and he's the man other trick-cyclists go to with their own problems or their patients' problems."

"So what?" Cripps said.

"He could be dangerous."

"You're talking rot, Mike," Cripps snapped. "I don't see how anybody can possible connect Whittaker's death on an East-London hospital slab with any of us. What d'you say, George?"

"Whittaker did come to the office just after he arrived," Wrigley said. "What if somebody spotted him?"

"Even if any of the old hands did, they wouldn't have recognized him as Matt," Cripps countered. "That face would have fooled his old mother if she'd been able to see."

"Didn't you both have a private visit?" Barnes queried. When the others nodded, the medical director clenched his fist. "He put the touch on the firm then on each of us, the bastard," he said.

"He didn't get much out of me," Cripps muttered.

Barnes kept silent and Wrigley looked embarrassed. "So what have the police got?" Cripps asked.

"If they unearthed all the records from more than twenty years ago …" Wrigley whispered in his dry, rasping voice.

"Everything was hidden," Cripps snapped.

"What about our own bank records?" the company secretary insisted. "They might wonder how we could deposit sizeable sums when we had a bankrupt firm on our hands."

"I don't see them doing that," the chairman came back.

"No, Wrigley's right," Barnes put in. "Especially if Whittaker carried out his threat and left a confession."

"Yes, he did mention a confession," Wrigley murmured. "Where would that be?"

"With that daughter of his," Barnes said. "She's still in this country and we've got to trace her and find out how much she's been told and what she's revealed to the police."

"That detective talked as though they knew everything," Wrigley commented. He seemed the most nervous of the trio.

"That's an old police dodge," Barnes said.

"I agree," Cripps said. "For instance, he can't possibly know who palmed the evidence on to the police dossier."

"The old lady might know something," Wrigley suggested. "Will they have seen her?"

"Get your wife to check that, Mike," Cripps ordered Barnes. "See what she can get out of that senile old baggage about who has seen her." Cripps drummed his manicured nails on his cigarette case, his greenish-blue eyes travelling from one to the other of his associates. "That leaves the surgeon who did

Whittaker's face. He might talk about us."

"I don't think so, somehow," Wrigley said. "He's got too much to lose now he's rich and famous."

"Yes, leave him out of it," Barnes said. "In my view it's only the Heredia girl we need worry about. We don't know if she has been told the full story by Whittaker or her mother. We've got to find out if she has a confession and what she might have told the police. Without that sort of evidence, the police haven't got a thing to convict us with."

"Where do we start hunting for her?" Wrigley asked.

"Well, we know she doesn't have police protection," Cripps said. "So, she must be hiding somewhere – probably with student friends or her mother's relatives. We can start there."

FIFTEEN

Maclean arrived at the St Andrews Clinic quarter of an hour after the operation began. They issued him with a green gown, a face-mask, a skull-cap and a pair of canvas overshoes before allowing him to step into the small theatre. Nobody paid any attention to him, for every pair of eyes was concentrating on that pool of light framing Mrs Woodruffe's oblivious face. To his surprise, Maclean noticed they had not started on the nose. Newcombe had evidently persuaded the lady to let him halve the number of her chins; he had made two long incisions just behind both sides of the jawbone and was paring away excess tissue with marvellous confidence and dexterity. They claimed he could manage eight to ten such operations in a day, and Maclean could see why; Newcombe plied those tiny, curved needles and silk suture like an expert seamstress. Of those surgeons whom the psychiatrist had watched, only Murdo Cameron would have matched that skill. So that he had Newcombe in profile he stood to one side, behind the anaesthetist. Anne Maxton had two trays of instruments deployed either side of her, one for general plastic work with its sets of forceps, scissors, hooks, retractors and probes, and the other for nasal surgery. No need to doubt that Newcombe and Maxton had collaborated on hundreds of operations; they had that telepathic understanding which develops between a surgeon and his theatre sister. Newcombe had turned to the nose and, as he finished examining its interior, she passed a small, spear-shaped scalpel and he expertly severed the skin from the two nasal bones, then carefully eased the flesh and bony structure apart. It looked very simple, but Maclean knew that few surgeons would have done it with such mastery. Another scalpel was slapped into his hand, this time with a saw blade; using this, Newcombe began sawing delicately through Mrs Woodruffe's prominent nasal bridge, withdrawing the bone fragments as he went.

When he had finished this, the surgeon muttered something unintelligible under his breath, then called for a wooden mallet and a sharp, semi-circular chisel; with these, he began to trim the sawed bone. Turning to pick up a second chisel, Sister Maxton let her glance fall on Maclean; those verdigris eyes widened as they ran over his bulky figure, then his face. Maclean could see her stiffen as she recognized him; her rubber-gloved hand grasped the chisel but, in her agitation, it spun out

of her hand to clatter on the tiled floor; she chose
another and her eyes dwelt on Newcombe's as he
looked askance at her; but he ignored the incident,
continuing to hammer and chisel the nasal bone. This
done, he spent ten minutes filing the bone with a rasp
while Sister Maxton was preparing a plaster of Paris
mixture to mould over the nose and fix its new shape.
Newcombe peeled off his gloves and tugged his
face-mask down as he walked towards the surgeon's
room. He was lighting a cigarette when he spotted
Maclean and his hand and the lighter halted for a split
second. "Ah! Maclean, I didn't know you were
interested in plastic surgery. What are you doing
here?"

"Just what every good doctor should do – follow his
patient into the operating theatre, or the morgue if
necessary."

"You're talking to a surgeon with nil mortality,"
Newcombe said with a grin. "And your patient won't
have any complications. She'll have a pair of black eyes
and a lovely conk for a week or ten days, then a new
nose to be proud of. If she's not a hundred per cent
satisfied, I'll give her back her money."

"I hope it cures her complex."

Newcombe peered at him with narrowed eyes. "You
weren't really worried about her," he said. "And you
didn't take time off just to look at nose-bobbing, did
you?"

"I must admit, I've never seen a top-flight *plastiqueur*
operate before," Maclean replied, avoiding the straight
answer. "It must give the ego a wonderful lift to
change somebody's face and their whole outlook in
under an hour."

Newcombe should have looked puzzled, but smiled
instead. "Those I change for the worse come after me

with a gun or leading a whole posse of lawyers. That keeps my ego in check."

"I remember the man with the gun," Maclean said. "Nobody ever tried to blackmail you?"

"Blackmail?" Now, the surgeon did look perplexed.

"In my trade, we've got to watch the psychopath who might stick a knife in our back. I can imagine one of your patients with a twisted mind threatening to drag you through the courts because your face didn't fit him, if you see what I mean."

"I'll watch my back," Newcombe said, leading the way into the surgeon's room. "Do you want to see your patient when she comes round?"

"No, but she might be difficult," Maclean murmured. "If you don't object I'll have a quiet word about her post-operative care with that remarkable theatre sister of yours, Sister Maxton."

Newcombe debated that. Untying his gown tapes, he slipped out of the garment and stood in nothing but a vest and short pants; he evidently kept himself in trim for he had a spare, hard body, his blue eyes had a healthy tinge and his face showed no sign of pouching or cross-hatching. A good ad for his trade, Maclean reflected. Newcombe reached into his locker for a cigarette case and lit another cigarette; he sucked deeply on the smoke, expelling it and glancing keenly at Maclean. He was no longer smiling. "Go ahead," he grunted. Thrusting his head round the door, he called, "Anne, I have Dr Gregor Maclean with me and he wants a word when you're done."

"I'm free now," she called back.

Apprehension clouded her face and those green eyes as she led him, mutely, to the nurses' office. She obviously remembered their brush in Whittaker's room and guessed what he wanted. However, for several minutes he kept the conversation on Mrs Woodruffe, her nose and face before saying, casually, "You worked for Sir Andrew Grant in the old days, didn't you?"

"For about a year," she replied. "Why?"

From a baggy pocket, Maclean drew out a crumpled envelope and dropped the two objects it contained into his palm. "Did Sir Andrew ever use this sort of gadget?" he asked, watching her gaze fix on the two coloured lenses like those Whittaker had worn.

"Contact lenses," she murmured.

"No," Maclean said. "They're the sort of thing eye surgeons use to treat conditions like albinism."

"I don't follow."

"Never mind," he said, leaving her puzzling while he produced another, larger envelope, from which he extracted a glossy picture of Whittaker. "Do you remember Sir Andrew or any of his assistants operating on this man?" he asked. Taking the picture, she gazed at it for several moments before shaking her head and handing it back. Maclean passed her the police photographs of Heredia. "Do you know him?" he queried.

"Yes," she said unhesitatingly. "He was a surgical patient in the East End Hospital, a case of perforating ulcer who died about a month ago on the operating table. He was a Spaniard, I think."

"But you must know – you attended the inquest on him."

"Yes, I did," she admitted, now flustered.

Maclean held up the pictures. "These two men were really the same man. Heredia was really an Englishman called Whittaker. He stole a fortune from the drug firm he ran and had an English plastic surgeon change his features, fit coloured contact lenses, then he fled abroad."

"What's all this got to do with me?" Anne Maxton asked.

"It happened just over twenty years ago when you were working for Sir Andrew Grant. These special lenses were ordered through Sir Andrew's surgical firm so it was probably he or one of his assistants who did the plastic surgery on Whittaker. I thought you might have an idea which one it was."

"Are you insinuating I might have assisted as such an operation?" Anne Maxton cried.

"No, Sister."

"Well, it's an absurd thing to suggest – that a surgeon would break the law by operating on a wanted man to change his face."

"Even if Whittaker tempted him," Maclean suggested. "He had a lot of money and some surgeon might have considered that, say twenty thousand pounds, was worth the risk of abetting a criminal and doing the surgery."

"I refuse to listen to any more of this slander," she snapped, pushing past him and hurrying along the corridor to the nurses' room.

Maclean pocketed his exhibits and strolled back to Harley Street. Newcombe had reacted much as he expected, calmly, though he obviously knew what Maclean's game was. Maxton, too, had kept cool while feigning anger at his suggestions. If, as he suspected, they were guilty, they would have to act now.

When he went through Deirdre's office, John Pearson was sitting hunched over two fish-and-chip suppers on paper plates which he was eating with a plastic knife and fork provided by Deirdre. Two empty Bass bottles stood by and he was drinking a third. "I'm on my way to a job the other side of the river, Mac, and I had to pay you a call."

"Something new?"

"Yes, they've taken me off Whittaker and put me back on my old beat. A gang slaying in Southwark. Two thugs who've done each other in. The kind we used to step over on the pavement and leave lying."

"How long will it take?"

"That doesn't matter," Pearson grunted. "When I've done it they'll hand me something else."

"Who's got the Whittaker case?"

"They've downgraded its priority and handed the file to a detective-constable called Marley."

"Who assigned you to the new job?"

"Dixon, the super who's my immediate boss."

"Any idea why?"

Pearson shook his head. "Probably some outside bigwig biting somebody's ear high up in the Yard," he muttered. He drank the last of his Bass, swallowed the froth off his moustache. "But you've got to go on, Mac. Just watch your back, that's all. From now on, I have to watch mine." He pecked Deidre on the cheek and stumped out. Maclean looked at Deirdre. "We're getting warm," he said.

SIXTEEN

Newcombe was standing at his office window watching the psychiatrist leave when Anne Maxton entered; she flopped into the easy chair and let out a long sigh. "That mental quack didn't come to admire your nose-bobbing and face-lifting technique," she said.

"You should have heard the questions he fired at me."
Taking a cigarette from the box on his desk, she lit it
and dragged deeply on it. "What does he know, I
wonder." Newcombe went to the drink cupboard to
mix them both a strong dose of gin and vermouth then
sat himself on the chair arm beside her. He placed a
hand on her shoulder and murmured, "Forget him,
darling. He's got absolutely nothing to go on – not a
smell of proof."

"But : told you I spotted him that morning in
Whittaker's room. And it was no mistake as he
pretended – he was searching for something."

"What, for instance?" Newcombe scoffed. "He was
merely snooping around trying to blame somebody
else for the blunder his protégé, Rothwell, made and
killed our man."

"Yes, but he's got some evidence now," she
countered. "Those funny contact lenses we fitted
Whittaker with and the photos of Whittaker and
Heredia. How did he get those?"

Newcombe hesitated. He had to calm her, prevent
her from doing something rash or panicking. "Take it
from me, Maclean's nowhere near answering the real
questions or he wouldn't be quizzing you," he said.
"He was just trying to scare me into confessing, or
running." Anne Maxton still looked troubled. He
kissed her lightly, then put out a hand to caress her
cheek and that point on her jawline where he had
excised her mole more than fifteen years before; it
titillated his vanity that even the hairline scar did not
show, so expertly had he welded the flesh together,
stitched and camouflaged it; at the same time he had
given her a pretty nose, *his* nose, the Newcombe nose
with a suspicion of a tip-tilt to throw the nostrils
slightly into relief and confer seduction to the face.

Amazing how a bit of subtle surgery could change a
face and character as it had done hers. In some strange
way it had made her his. But then he felt he had put his
stamp on all those women who had come begging him
to revise nature's failings, correct her errors and turn
the clock back. Newcombe could admire again and
again his handiwork with the fond eye of the artist and
creator. He ran his hand over Anne Maxton's face,
then held her glass to her lips until it was empty.

Her green eyes tracked him to the drink cupboard.
She had known him ever since he arrived, a callow
young surgeon, to learn plastic surgery at Sir Andrew
Grant's elbow when she was a budding theatre nurse.
Then he had asked her to work with him. All surgeons
had to pick good nurses, but none more so than plastic
surgeons; even after perfect operations, their patients
had a harrowing time until the bruising subsided and
they had rediscovered their new faces or figures; and
for those patients where things had gone wrong, a
good nurse had to act like a psychiatrist, pacifying,
calming, reassuring. All this she had done for
Newcombe when he set up in private practice, then in
Harley Street. As he mixed fresh drinks she studied
him. Physically he had scarcely changed; he still had a
slim, athletic body and smooth face. Anne Maxton
thought back to the sacrifices she had made for him.
She had been in love with him and his mistress for
three years, but he had never felt her good enough to
marry; theirs had always been a professional affair, for
he had always treated her like his nurse, a willing pair
of hands. Perhaps had she acted less like the good
theatre sister ... Could she have held him? Kept pace
with his high-flying ambitions? Her gaze shifted to the
portraits of celebrities he had operated on, then to
studio portrait sitting apart on his desk – a dark-eyed

woman with swept-back, dark hair and an oval Modigliani face. She had come to have her nose bobbed and wrinkles stretched – but he had married her. After all, she was Vivienne Manning, an international stage and film star with a hieratic presence, a walking advertisement for him. She had her debit side. Newcombe had to earn enough to pay her mink and jewels and lavish parties and keep three houses and a yacht going. Now they whispered that her age difference – she was two years older – was beginning to show and she was playing the role of the ageing actress, jealous of her husband's success. Yet nothing of this ever passed across Newcombe's bland face; he never spoke of his home life.

She accepted the drink from him and he murmured, "The mixture as before – ten centilitres of gin and ten millilitres of dry vermouth."

For several minutes they sat in silence before she spoke. "I often wonder what would have happened to you if you hadn't done that operation on Whittaker," she murmured.

"I'd have been a lot poorer."

"You'd still have made the top as a plastic surgeon."

"Probably on my last legs."

"But it was a tremendous risk you took."

"It's a risky job, and it was a calculated risk," he replied. "When could I have hoped to set up my plate in Harley Street without that money?"

"What could they do now – if they found out, I mean?"

"Shove me in clink for aiding and abetting a criminal before and after the fact."

"For how long?"

"A year to eighteen months if they go by the facts alone, and nine months with a brilliant lawyer," he muttered. He gulped a mouthful of liquor and grimaced at her. "But what I would get and when I came out wouldn't matter to me. All those nice black-jacketed colleagues along Harley Street and those splendid hospital consultants would rip me up and share out my patients after the General Medical Council hd struck me off. I'd be no good to anybody."

"But your wife – she'd stand by you?"

"Maybe yes and maybe no," Newcombe grunted. He knew where that conversation was heading and cut it short. "Look, sweetheart, nobody will land in jail and be blackballed because nobody's going to find out about that little episode. There was only you and me and our dead friend, Whittaker, in that private house, so who's to guess?"

Ann Maxton's mind recalled that private house near Basingstoke where she had lived for nine long weeks with Whittaker as her sole patient; she had assisted Newcombe when he performed the operations in a back bedroom converted into a makeshift surgery; she had nursed Whittaker and fed him and driven him to the coast when he caught his boat for exile with his new passport and a new face.

"And the others in the know?" she queried.

"They've got too much to lose – like me." Newcombe emptied his glass, reached out for her hand and pulled her to her feet. "Come on, let's go to your flat, you can change and I'll buy you a bite in the West End and we'll take in a show." Amazed, he watched her shake her head when normally she would have leapt at the offer.

"I don't think we should be seen together – for a bit, anyway," she murmured.

"You mean until we've got Maclean and his friends

off our backs?" She nodded, and he said, "Maybe you're right."

SEVENTEEN

Anne Maxton spotted him in a corner of the Mitre as she entered the saloon bar. He was drinking a half-pint of bitter ale, a bad sign for a serious drinker. Assuming her best smile, she walked over and when he rose, kissed him on the cheek, then on the lips. She took a seat on the lounge sofa behind him. "Where have you got to?" she asked. "I had a devil of a job to get a message to you."

"I had a row with my landlord and had to get out in a hurry," Rothwell said. "He changed the lock on my door without giving me time to look round." He discerned scepticism in her glance.

"Anyway, I'm glad the ground-floor gargoyle contacted you," she said. "Where are you living now?"

"I'm digging with a family until I can find another flat," he said. "They're hard to come by, and pricey, and I'm hard up."

"That's why I thought you might be interested in earning a bit of extra money at the clinic. It's private work and they pay £100 a morning session to whoever gives the anaesthetics."

Rothwell looked at her. In a crêpe-silk dress and high-heeled shoes, with a mink wrap over her shoulders, she looked pretty and seductive and it flattered him that she had not only found him a job but had spent time and effort dolling herself up for him. When she crossed those elegant legs, he saw the men at the bar eyeing her; none of them would ever have taken her for a theatre sister. "Who's operating and what on?" he asked.

"Three *plastiqueurs* who take it in turn nose-bobbing, face-lifting, breast-lifting – beauty parlour stuff. There's Newcombe, Crozier and Ralston-Smith. Newcombe knows you and I told the others how good you are on low-blood-pressure anaesthetics." She glanced at his half-empty beer mug and grimaced with disgust. "You're not going to stay on that stuff, are you?"

Rothwell hesitated for a moment, then shook his head, asking her what she wanted. When she said a double gin and tonic, he crossed to the bar and brought back two double gins and two tonics. She drank hers quickly then beckoned to the barman to fetch the same again. "Where'd you like to eat?" Rothwell asked.

Anne Maxton looked at the tiny, jewelled watch dangling from her breast. "But we've got loads of time," she laughed. "I've had a hard day in theatre with Newcombe and I need to wind down a bit." She threaded an arm through his and snuggled up to him. "Why did we ever fall out, Philip?" she murmured in his ear. She let her mink wrap drop over the back of the settle to reveal half of her firm breasts. "I've missed you. Have you missed me?"

Rothwell nodded. He realized he should have risen and fled, yet he was weak and this woman knew that. But what the hell! She had found him a job. He had to be gallant. However, he did not intend to have more than a couple of drinks with Anne Maxton; he reckoned to meet and thank her and get back quickly to the flat where he had left Maria on her own. But somehow after the fourth drink Anne Maxton became more and more alluring and his resolve collapsed. Soon, the idea of having a meal somewhere evaporated and he had lost track of how much he was drinking, only that the rounds of double gins were repeating faster and faster. When the pub threw them out just after eleven he discovered he was really drunk; the night air set his head reeling and he was walking on feathers. Anne Maxton hung on to him and flagged a cab to take them to her flat in Belgravia.

Rothwell flopped on to the sofa in her elegant living-room. He knew the flat well and in his more sober moments had often wondered how she managed to pay the rent of a whole floor of this Georgian building in a chic London district, even though she did earn top money working for half a dozen private surgeons as well as in her hospital.

Anne Maxton had discarded her mink wrap and kicked of her shoes before going to mix them more drinks. Looking over her shoulder at Rothwell, she decided not to spike his drink; he seemed far enough gone. She joined Rothwell on the sofa and clinked her glass with his.

"I've got to get back," he said, thickly.

"What's the hurry?" she whispered. "You can stay here the night." She giggled. "Of course you'd have to share my double bed."

"No, Anne," he protested. But already she was undressing him, running her sharp-pointed nails gently over his chest knowing this set him going sexually. She allowed him to fumble with the hooks and zips of her dress and her bra, stifling her annoyance at the time he was taking. She tried, half-heartedly, to draw him towards the bedroom, finally yielding to his resistance. Although she had powerful sexual impulses, Anne Maxton had little urge to make love with Rothwell and had to drive her will. "Here – on the sofa," Rothwell croaked. Drugged by too much alcohol, Rothwell made love merely to save face and it took all her talent to bring him to his climax. When he rolled over and lay, spent, on the sofa she covered him with a travelling rug and waited until he was snoring.

In one of his jacket pockets, she found what she sought – two bunches of keys. One she knew for his flat keys and put them back. Those other two keys, for a patent and a mortice lock, must belong to the flat where he was now living, the one he was so cagey about. Going into the kitchen, she melted and mixed some dental wax and made two careful impressions of each key, then wiped them carefully before returning them to Rothwell's pocket. She set her alarm clock for three and lay down in a bathrobe on her bed. When the clock woke her, she went to rouse Rothwell. "Philip, it's time to go home," she said.

Rothwell gazed, bleary-eyed, at the carriage clock on the mantelpiece. "After three," he muttered. "I'll get shot." While he retrieved his clothes and dressed, she called a mini-cab from the company she used herself. "Wha'd I have to drink tonight?" he asked as she helped him downstairs to the cab. "Too much, darling," she laughed.

He had enough wit left to order the cab-driver to take him to Holland Park where he had left his own car; but she vetoed this, warning him he would run into a police patrol at this hour and lose his licence. Rothwell then gave his old address and waited until the cab had turned the corner before directing the driver to Nelson Mews. Anne Maxton saw through his subterfuge. When she went back upstairs, she rang the cab company to say her friend had left something important in her flat. Would they kindly send the cab-driver back to see her?

When he arrived at the door of the flat, Rothwell had recovered his senses enough to give Maria's special knock. Even then, she crept downstairs in her nightdress and called to him. When he identified himself, she opened the door fraction by fraction to check he had no one with him. He tried to stammer a drunken excuse but gave up. Maria would never have understood that being thrown so closely together in this flat had something to do with his lapse tonight. She did not chide him or say anything, but then she had no need. Her frightened face said everything.

EIGHTEEN

Over the weekend, Maclean dissected and analyzed every note he had written on the Whittaker Case. Again and again, he read those dog-eared papers in the Yard dossier and the sere newspaper cuttings until his eyes filmed over with fatigue. He had an unshakeable conviction the same person had killed both Whittaker and his wife and must belong to that quartet of Ronald Cripps, Michael Barnes, George Wrigley and Robert Randal Newcombe. And somehow, Maxton was also involved. Always, Maclean came back to that one vital part of their plot: who had palmed the medical evidence in the police files to convince Scotland Yard

Whittaker had really died? And why did Whittaker have to go to immense trouble and expense to kill himself off on paper? Solve those questions and he had the murderer. Once more, Maclean gazed at those pictures of the hotel fire and the detectives who had investigated it. Inspector Bernard Carpenter, who had led the inquiry, was dead. But where were the others in those photos? One man might know, the police surgeon for that Notting Hill district – Dr Jacob Gould.

On Monday afternoon, a selection of newspaper cuttings in his pocket, Maclean took a cab to Holland Park and knocked on Gould's door. "Jake, I need some help," he said.

"If you're in bad with the law or the General Medical Council for any or all of the Six As, I'll prescribe and dispense you a black coffee and send you on your way," Gould said on his doorstep.

"The Six As?"

"Advertizing, Abortion, Adultery, Addiction, Alcohol and Assault."

"No, Jake, this is about a patient's problem."

"Well, I suppose I've sent a few to you in my day," Gould muttered.

He opened the door to admit Maclean, then conducted him through to his study where he lifted a heap of medical journals and magazines off an easy chair and placed them on a desk that was piled high with the books and papers he had been studying.

Gould excused himself for the mess. He gently shooed a black cat off an easy chair and a marmalade cat off his own swivel seat and invited the psychiatrist to sit down. Gould knew everyone and everything in the district; he still acted as a police surgeon as well as heading the local British Medical Association committee and running an extensive private and state practice; he had a bald head, a jowly, pouchy face, muddy, myopic eyes, and his stomach overspilled his waistband. Maclean had know him for twenty years and handled him cannily, for Gould was as wily as a bagful of rats. Carefully he expounded his story, which sounded thinner than when he had rehearsed it: a patient of his had an obsessive and recurrent dream that her father, who had disappeared twenty years ago, was still alive. So vivid and frequent was this dream, the woman felt it had to be true; it haunted her to the point where she began to suffer from depression and she had come to beg Maclean to exorcise the dream and restore her peace of mind. He had done neither. After months of treatment, he had decided to try to trace her father or at worst prove him dead. "I've narrowed the inquiry down to the two weeks he spent in London before disappearing, Jake," the psychiatrist said. "He was in this area." Behind his bottle lenses and hooded lids, Gould's eyes were scanning him and Maclean sensed the general practitioner placed no credence whatever in this sort of psychiatry, less in dreams and hardly any in Maclean's tale.

"You want a Ouija board or an astrologer, Mac," he grunted.

"My patient traced her father to a hotel on the fringes of Bayswater and Notting Hill," Maclean said, ignoring the jibe. "He moved from there without paying his bill – presumably to another hotel." From a pocket, he produced a small envelope of newspaper cuttings and smoothed out those dealing with the Ladbrook Hotel fire. "I thought it might be this one," he said.

Gould thrust his glasses up over his wrinkled forehead and held the cuttings close to his nose. "I know it," he muttered. "Ladbrook Hotel – sleazy little pad – five people died and three were so badly charred it took weeks to identify them." Gould peered hard at Maclean. "But one of them was identified. Weren't the police interested in him?"

"Yes, there was a man called Whittaker, a company director who'd absconded with the till," Maclean admitted.

"Not only the till – there was a drug angle," Gould murmured, taking off his thick glasses, half-swallowing, then polishing, them. "Wasn't he flogging purple hearts and the like?"

Maclean shrugged, trying not to betray his interest in what Gould had revealed. "I wouldn't know," he said. "It's the two unidentified men that interest me."

"So, how can I help you, Mac?"

"Who was the police surgeon then?"

"Stephen Jackson – dead these ten years." Gould scanned the cuttings again, pointing to the three detectives in the rubble of the hotel basement. "Carpenter's dead." His tuberous finger landed on the second Yard man. "He's dead, too – name of Fred Holton. He was a detective-sergeant on that job and finished as head man over at Harrow Road."

"And the other man?"

"No idea," Gould said. "He couldn't have had much rank."

"If he's alive I'd like to have a word with him," Maclean remarked. "It'd be a big favour, Jake, if you could get his name for me."

"Have you asked the Yard?"

"You know what the Yard is for not saying anything."

"Is it that important?"

"A woman's life and happiness may depend on it."

Gould proffered a pudgy hand. Knowing how much he liked a pinch of strong snuff, Maclean produced his ebony box; for several minutes they both snuffed and snorted like two bulls in a pen. Gould trumpeted through his nose and swabbed his eyes. "Might take a day or two to run somebody down at Notting Hill who remembers the fire and knew that copper," he wheezed. Again, he held out his hand and the psychiatrist built another mound of snuff on the back of it. When Gould had subsided, he picked up a couple of newspaper cuttings. "Can I hang on to these for a couple of days?" he asked.

"Don't flash them around to much," Maclean replied.

He strolled back to his flat and put through a call to Maria, who assured him everything was fine. Rothwell had a session at a private clinic the next morning, but she would stay in the flat with all the doors locked and chained. Maclean was working again through his Whittaker file when Deirdre returned with a bulky envelope full of glossy photographs which she threw on the sofa beside him. She had spent all afternoon at two London teaching hospitals weeding through piles of group pictures of nurses to find those with Anne Maxton as a probationer and later as a fully trained theatre sister. Quickly, he ran his gaze over the pictures, singling out Maxton from the collections of uniformed nurses, studying her companions closely and reading off the list of names Deirdre had compiled; he was seeking any clue to connect Maxton, Newcombe and Whittaker's old associates.

"I found out who carved the mole off her face, the bead off her snout, and made her look like the angel with the lamp," she said.

"Our friend Newcombe," he suggested.

"Who else?"

"You know what that means," he said. "Newcombe

thinks when he's remade their faces, he can make them."

"There he wouldn't get his eyes scratched out."

Maclean suddenly beckoned her over. "You said she'd hardly any friends." He held up an early picture, taken before Maxton had asked Newcombe to change her features; she was wearing probationer's uniform and was standing in a group of about twenty other young nurses; she had her arm round a pretty, dark-haired nurse who, in turn, was embracing Maxton round the waist. "Who's she?" Maclean queried.

"I knew you'd ask that, but I don't know," Deirdre said. That picture had come from a nurse in the group, now a ward sister, and she could not remember the girl. However, she thought the girl had not remained in the profession long. "I'm getting the East End and two other hospitals to search through their records for that year," Deirdre said.

"Hurry them up," he said. "It may be important."

They had finished their evening meal when the phone rang Deirdre picked up the instrument, cupped her hand over the mouthpiece. "It's Dr Gould," she whispered.

"Mac, you owe me at least half a pound of that decapitating snuff of yours," Jake Gould said in his gravelly baritone.

"Who was he?"

"Somebody who's climbed to the top at the Yard. I should've spotted him myself, for I met him when he was at Notting Hill as a detective constable."

"What's his name?"

"Crowther – Frank Crowther, and he's a chief superintendent with a couple of dozen detectives under him." Gould lowered his voice. "Don't tell him I told you."

"You're sure it's him on that picture?"

"Sure I'm sure," Gould insisted. "As plug-ugly then as he is now. Worse than me."

"Thanks, Jake," Maclean said, putting down the phone.

Frank Crowther! Maclean could not believe he had anything to do with the Whittaker business. He knew something about the man from press articles and his appearance on TV. Something of a Yard legend, he had solved dozens of famous crimes, among them the so-called Vampire Murders, committed by a mousy insurance agent who claimed to have sucked the blood of his women victims after strangling them. Just as celebrated was his handling of a racing coup by a betting syndicate which had flown in a 'dead ringer' from Ireland to replace a slow selling-plate at Ayr races in 1975. They stood to clear half a million pounds when their 'ringer' won by ten lengths. However, Crowther broke the case by interviewing more than five hundred people before tracing and identifying the 'ringer' by its racing plates, their nails and its harness. Conviction of the six-man betting syndicate made his name and since then he had moved up to become one of the Yard's senior chief superintendents. How could a man like that get mixed up in the Whittaker crimes? It must either be one of the dead detectives, or Jake Gould had mistaken his man. However, somebody in the Yard had not only planted evidence in the Whittaker file but had gone back to the archives and cleaned out anything that might incriminate him. But would he or anybody else ever prove it?

NINETEEN

Rothwell glanced at the clock. Quarter to nine. Gulping the rest of his coffee, he rose and collected his coat and cap then the medical bag in which he kept his own anaesthetic kit. "Maria, are you sure you don't mind being left alone for a morning?" he asked. She shook her head, murmuring that he must go and do the session he had promised. He picked up the shopping list she had compiled and stuffed it in a pocket. "I'll be back just after twelve-thirty," he said. He looked at her with a contrite face. "You're not still sore at me, are you?"

"No, I wasn't angry – just scared out of my wits," she replied. "I thought somebody might have killed you this time."

Rothwell had hardly put a foot outside the flat since he had returned, drunk, three nights before. But he had given Anne Maxton and Newcombe his word to administer anaesthetics at the St Andrews Clinic that morning. To reassure Maria, he had gone to a local ironmonger's and bought a thicker door chain which he had fixed in addition to the existing one for greater security.

Maria saw him downstairs to the front door. "I'll put both chains on and I shall not answer to anyone," she said.

"If anything happens or anybody tries to get in, ring

Dr Mac or Deirdre at their consulting-room," he said.
On the doorstep he paused, then kissed her first on the
cheek, then on the lips. She watched him walk round
the corner to his car before locking and chaining the
door. Upstairs, she poured herself more coffee and
sipped it. Her cheek and lips still tingled where Philip
had kissed her. What did Philip think of her? Probably
that she was stupid and naïve and years younger than
her age. He was right. In Spain and almost everywhere
else, she had always lived with her parents and they had
good reason not to make friends or encourage her to
go with boys. Apart from one or two parties and casual
meetings, she had no experience of men. But she felt
drawn to Philip. Deidre had told her his story, but she
did not seem to realize how lonely and isolated
somebody like Philip could be. Maria understood that,
having been lonely all her life. Philip was kind, too
kind, and people had preyed on him. He had respected
her sorrow and her old-fashioned ideas and had not
tried to take advantage of their situations. One person,
she thought, did understand him: Dr Maclean.

When she had drunk her coffee and tidied up the
kitchen and living-room, Maria went into the
bathroom adjoining her own bedroom and had a
shower. For quarter of an hour she let hot and cold
water sluice over her body. Towelling herself down,
she wrapped a bathrobe round her and stepped out of
the bathroom. At that moment, a gloved hand reached
out and clamped over her nose and mouth. A voice
hissed in her ear. "If you scream. I shall kill you."
Maria saw the glint of something in his other hand
and, to her horror, realized it was a long-bladed knife
pressed against her heart. He released his hand and she
took a deep breath. "Don't talk – just get dressed –
quickly," he commanded. Shivering with fear, Maria

gathered her underwear, suit, stockings and shoes and began to dress, conscious of his eyes on her back. When she had finished dressing, he ordered, "Sit down," and pointed to a chair. She complied. He took the cord of her bathrobe, pulled her wrists forward and bound them tightly together. From the wardrobe he took one of her coats and placed it over her tied hands to make it look as if she were carrying it that way. "Now, if you scream or attempt to attract attention to us, I shall shoot you," he said. To reinforce this threat, he produced a heavy automatic pistol from his coat pocket, then put it back.

Maria eyed him. She had no doubt this was the man who had attacked her at Rothwell's flat then tried to break in. He wore the same sort of coat and hat and kept his face half-hidden in a woollen scarf. Yet, his grizzling hair showed. And those funny blue eyes, the colour of dark gunmetal had a sterile glitter; he glared at her through narrowed eyelids as though he were myopic.

"You will walk slightly ahead of me to my car, looking neither to the right or to the left. Understood?" His voice had a clipped, metallic quality and sounded sinister. Maria did not doubt that this man had murdered her mother as well. When he prompted her with a gesture she rose and preceded him downstairs. There, she realized how he had got in – by cutting through the two door chains with heavy wire-cutters that lay in the hallway. But how had he opened the door to cut the chain? How had he acquired the flat keys? "My car is the black one just beyond the mews entrance," he said, prodding her outside.

Her mouth had gone dry, her heart was thumping in her chest and her legs felt watery. Where was he taking her? That neutral voice grated, "Open the front door and get in. Don't try to run or I'll kill you." Maria could hardly walk, let alone think of running. She fumbled with the door lock, finally managing to open the door and take her seat. He came round quickly, threw the cutters which he had hidden in his coat on to the back seat and slipped behind the wheel. As he drove through the back streets leading to Notting Hill Gate, she had a chance to glance at him. He had smooth, grey features. High up on his left cheek-bone, level with his ear, he had a wine-stain birthmark shaped like a sombrero with a ragged brim. She would remember that, and those peculiar eyes that she noticed again when he flicked a glance in the rear mirror. But remember for how long, she wondered.

"What have you told the police about your father?" he asked abruptly.

"What I knew."

"That was foolish of you," he commented. He turned that lifeless stare on her. "Of course it depends how many of the secrets you were told."

"Enough," she said.

"You knew what and who he was? And your mother?"

"They told me as soon as I was old enough to understand."

"He was a fool, your father."

"He was – to trust you and let you murder him and my mother."

"A pity nobody but you and your psychiatrist friend believe that story."

They had reached the end of Church Street and he steered the black sedan into Kensington High Street. There he had to concentrate on the road with its lights and pedestrian crossings. Maria was thinking. This cold-blooded man was going to murder her where and when it suited her. She must act. But if she made any move to get out of the car, he would stun her or would not hesitate to kill her. What could she do? Something flashed across her mind. Before he had started the car away from the kerbside at the mews, he had to wrestle with the steering-wheel to free it from its locked position. Her father had once owned a car like this and it had run away with the steering-wheel locked and nearly killed him. Desperately, she tried to remember how that had happened. Hadn't it something to do with the ignition key and starter? Of course, the wheel locked when the car was stationary – when the ignition key was withdrawn! Without turning her head, Maria scanned the dashboard for the key. It lay just under the wheel on the steering column. That was difficult. She would have to reach out with both her bound hands, seize it, pull it out, then spin round, open the door and flee. She must therefore choose her moment and leave him wondering what had happened. Slowly, she let the coat slip through her arms and fall between her legs. They had come up to Earls Court where the lights halted them. It was the moment to act. Perhaps the only one.

As the lights changed and the big car accelerated and began to turn left, Maria shoved her two hands to the right, snatched the key and threw it behind her. Both front wheels locked on a left-hand turning position, the vehicle spun round with the driver struggling vainly with the locked steering-wheel trying to straighten the car. It hit the high kerb with a bang and Maria caught sight of a dozen pedestrians scattering from its path and heard others screaming a warning. As the man beside her stepped on the brakes Maria braced herself against the shock. Then she slammed the door catch down with both hands, put her shoulder to the door and, as it flew open, sprang out. Without looking round, she sprinted for the corner and turned into Kensington High Street waving frantically to every cab that passed. One stopped and she jumped in, shouting at the driver to take her to Harley Street. When he turned, she glanced fearfully through the rear window and saw a crowd had already collected at the entrance to Earls Court Road.

At Harley Street, she managed to climb the stairs to Maclean's consulting-room before the nightmare of what she had experienced caught up with her and she fainted.

TWENTY

Maclean cancelled his list for the rest of the day and cleared his consulting-room to let Maria lie down on his couch with Deirdre looking after her. He phoned the clinic where Rothwell was working and ordered him to take a cab to Harley Street when he had finished his duty. He also managed to track Pearson down through the Southwark police station and asked him to come urgently to the consulting-room.

When Rothwell arrived, Maclean thrust him, unceremoniously, into the consulting-room, closed the double door and steered him through the penumbral gloom to where Maria was lying. "This is the girl you were supposed to protect," he snapped. "She's just escaped being murdered again."

Rothwell listened, mutely, to his account of Maria's ordeal, then shook his head, sadly. "It's my fault," he got out. He related how he had met Maxton and she had lured him back to her flat, got him drunk and had obviously found the mews address from the taxi-driver. Maclean glared at him and brandished a huge fist. Never had Deirdre seen him so furious. Despite the sound-proofing, his voice boomed.

"And she took copies of the two keys you were carrying and passed them on to her murdering accomplice for him to finish the job," he said. "I don't know why I bother with poor types like you."

"Gregor," Deirdre began, but he quietened her with a glance.

Maria looked up from her couch at the psychiatrist. "Dr Maclean," she said. "Philip told me about the other night and it wasn't all his fault. Anyway, as a psychiatrist, you must know what he has been through."

Maclean glowered, then pointed at Rothwell. "People like him make me forget I'm a psychiatrist," he said. "I ought to have him locked up as an accessory to attempted murder."

"But if I have forgiven him, why cannot you?" the girl pleaded.

In the gloom of the consulting-room Deirdre could not have sworn to it, but Maclean appeared to wink at her when he turned to speak to Maria, as though his outburst had been calculated. "All right," he conceded, "I'll forgive him this time – but if he goes off the rails again he's on his own."

"Thank you, Dr Maclean," Maria murmured.

"Yes, thanks, Gregor," Rothwell said.

Deirdre brewed them instant coffee and sent the receptionist out for sandwiches while they waited for

John Pearson to arrive. He joined them in the office just before one o'clock and listened while Maclean described Maria's experience and the part Maxton had played in the attempt to kill the girl.

"So we rope in Maxton and Newcombe and ask them a few questions," Pearson suggested.

Maclean demolished that notion. "We don't know for certain the man who attacked Maria is Newcombe. And even if we suspected him, he probably has a friend if not an accomplice in your building."

Pearson gave him a hard, searching look. "Have you got proof?" he asked.

"Not absolute proof," Maclean replied. "How well do you know Chief Superintendent Frank Hurst Crowther?"

"Not well, but he's one of the best detectives in the history of the Yard," Pearson said.

"In your opinion, he couldn't possibly be the nark who tipped off the man who murdered Maria's mother?"

"Not a chance."

"Then it'll do no harm if you help to prove he's got nothing to do with the plot," Maclean said.

Pearson shook his head. "I'm a copper, Mac, and I want to stay a copper."

"But all I want you to do, John, is stand in the information room and watch what happens when Maria here phones the Yard and tells the truth by saying somebody's trying to murder her, then asks for police protection."

Deirdre could not contain herself at this. "But it's monstrous!" she cried. "After what she's been through I'm not going to allow you to put this girl's life at risk again."

Maclean put his arm round her and smiled. "Don't worry, mavournin, you're going to stand in for her and play the part of the decoy."

"Me!" Deirdre gasped, blanching at the thought. "I could never do that."

"I'll write you a splendid script."

"And the funeral oration, too," she said.

Maclean explained his plan. Maria would stay in this consulting-room with Rothwell while he and Deirdre would book a room in a small hotel a mile or two away in case the Yard information room had to ring back to confirm the girl's story.

"You really think this call will be picked up by somebody in the Yard and relayed to the murderer," Pearson said.

"That's the theory."

Pearson shrugged. For himself, he failed to understand how they were ever going to pinpoint the leak from the Yard where there were literally hundreds of phone lines busy every minute and dozens of private phones for the top men. And if they posted Maria's message on the information-room board, anybody could spot it and ring from an outside box without fear of discovery. "Unless you put the whole of the Yard on a wire-tap you haven't a hope of catching the nark if there is one."

"I have a smell about Crowther."

"Even then, how do you trap him?"

"Somebody like you rings him on his private number and absent-mindedly forgets to put the phone back, and that puts Crowther's phone out of commission and he has to use the switchboard."

"He could use another office."

"Too risky," Maclean came back.

"All right, an outside call-box."

"In a district bristling with nosy coppers who might remember one of their chief superintendents."

Pearson stubbed out his cigarette and gave an exasperated wave of his hand. "Why do I even listen to a clansman like you, Mac? If you're right, I'm doing the Yard down, and if you're wrong I'm back flatfooting in the London dockland."

"If I'm right you'll get a detective division all to yourself."

Maclean briefed everyone, then rehearsed them in their parts before they split up. Pearson took him aside as he left. "From the girl's description, it looked like Cripps or Newcombe. Do you think I should alert the local stations?"

"No, do nothing until we know for sure who the murderer is."

"Who do you think?"

Maclean looked at the detective and shrugged. "I honestly couldn't make a guess," he said.

A couple of hours later, Deirdre drove Maclean to Shepherd's Bush where she was going to book into the Holland Lodge Hotel. He sensed her apprehension and tried to reassure her, though disguising the fact that he, too, felt queasy at the idea of exposing her to someone to had already murdered twice. "You'll be all right," he said. "John has detailed two men from Notting Hill to protect you and I'll be hiding with one of them in the room."

"What if he shoots first?"

"And kills the best secretary, psychiatrist, cook, helpmeet and soul-mate that I could ever hope to have," he exclaimed. "If he did that I'd strangle him with my bare hands, having nothing left to live for."

Deirdre took her eye off the road to stare at him, wondering as she did for half her life, whether to take him seriously or not. Finally, she said, "You know, Dr

Alexander Gregor Maclean, sometimes I wonder if it's catching and you've caught it."

"What's catching?"

"The sort of madness you treat on your couch or in your hospital."

"But it is, didn't you know?" he said. "That's why the daily woman has orders to spray the room and disinfect the couch with carbolic acid."

"I meant what about me, what about my life?" she cried, banging on the steering-wheel in her exasperation.

"I'll have her spray your office, desk and things if you're worried," he said, blandly misinterpreting her meaning.

Deirdre gave up. They were approaching Shepherd's Bush and she left the small Fiat some distance from their destination. Although Maclean had chosen the hotel because he knew the proprietor they could not take the chance that someone might spot Deirdre entering the place. She walked there alone. Pearson's two plain-clothes policemen were already there, and Maclean would join one of them in Deirdre's room in an hour's time while the other watched the area around the hotel.

TWENTY-ONE

John Pearson was keeping an eye on the clock in his Scotland Yard office. When it came to five minutes to five, he picked up the private phone in his office and dialled Chief Superintendent Frank Crowther's private number five floors above him. He heard the husky, gravelly voice bark several hallos into the mouthpiece then the click as Crowther replaced the receiver. Pearson had already stuck bits of sticky tape over the cradle of his phone to keep the receiver off the contacts. Since he was maintaining an open line through to Crowther's private number, the Yard chief could not use it. At just after five, Pearson locked his office and left the fifth floor – his normal routine when he was working from headquarters. If everything went as planned, he could remove the tape and restore the phone before the cleaners made their round.

Pearson took the lift down to the information room. In ten minutes, the call would come through from Maria Heredia and that gave him time to scan the notice-board and teleprinters with their usual crop of accidents, holdups, lorry hijackings. His eyes halted on the report of the car crash Maria Heredia had provoked in Earls Court Road late that morning. They had listed the Black Austin sedan as a stolen car because the driver and passenger had run from the crash scene and the registration plates were false; they had not yet succeeded in tracing the owner.

"Anything we can do for you, John?" Pearson turned to find the sergeant who had just come on duty at his elbow. He pointed to the crash report.

"I was interested in this one. The girl who ran away had her hands bound according to witnesses. It looked to us like an abduction or a hostage case. If you get anything ..."

"We'll let you know," the sergeant said, then headed for his desk with its half-dozen coloured telephones which sat between two radio transmitters.

At five-fifteen, Pearson was pretending to take notes

off one teleprinter report when the sergeant hailed
him. "This might be yours, John. It's a girl, a foreigner
by the sound, says she was kidnapped at gunpoint and
somebody tried to kill her for the second time." He
pointed to one of the coloured phones and Pearson
walked over to pick it up. Maria was doing splendidly,
describing in breathless, accented English how she had
been threatened with a knife and a gun and her hands
bound before she was driven to Kensington. She had
caused the accident to escape from the man. He had
already tried to strangle her and she was sure he had
murdered her mother.

At this the sergeant grimaced with surprise and
signalled to John to take notes. "What did you say your
name was, miss?" he asked. "Heredia – Maria
Heredia. My father's name was Whittaker, Matthew
Whittaker. He stole a large sum of money many years
ago."

"Where are you speaking from and what's your
number there?"

"The Holland Lodge Hotel in Shepherd's Bush. The
number is 994 2622."

"Hold on a minute. Don't go away now." While he
had been speaking, the sergeant was consulting a list by
his elbow. He shouted to the switchboard, "Put me
through to Chief Superintendent Crowther." Aside to
Pearson he whispered, "He's got a special interest in
this case it seems." Pearson was still monitoring the
call; he heard Crowther come on and the sergeant
repeat everything the girl had just said. Crowther
instructed the sergeant not to retransmit the message
on the police network as he would take care of it
himself. Connected at his request with Maria Heredia,
he did not introduce himself, but cross-examined her
at length and told her to stay where she was until

someone came and picked her up in a police car. On no account must she move.

Pearson had heard enough. Putting down the phone, he moved across to the switchboard where he watched the electronic buttons, waiting for Crowther's extension to show on them. When it did, he pointed to it and his ear, indicating to the constable operating the board he would like to eavesdrop. Unsuspecting, the man handed him his spare phone on the board. Pearson picked up the ringing tone as soon as Crowther had dialled the number. A woman's voice said, "Hallo." Crowther did not waste words, murmuring simply and naturally, "She's at the Holland Lodge Hotel, Shepherd's Bush – room number twenty-three."

"Shall I tell Anne and Bob?"

"No need," Crowther said and put down the phone.

Pearson went upstairs to his own office to remove the tape and replace the receiver. That call from Crowther had confirmed all Maclean's suspicions and the big detective wondered if he should stay and keep an eye on the superintendent. But what if more than one man turned up at the hotel and anything happened to Deirdre and the psychiatrist? Pearson hurried downstairs and out to his own car and drove to Shepherd's Bush. There, he alerted both his men, placing them outside the hotel. He reported what had happened at the Yard to Maclean. "Who's the woman Crowther phoned?" he asked. "Maxton?"

"Probably a friend of hers."

"And Bob?"

"Newcombe, most likely."

"We should put out an arrest call for them."

Maclean shook his head. "It would alert Crowther,"

he said. "And we don't know yet whether Newcombe isn't the killer."

From Deirdre's room they took turns watching the roads leading into the square. For nearly two hours nothing happened. Then, at seven-thirty as it was growing dark, Deirdre spotted the black sedan drawing up in Uxbridge Road. A man got out, but he seemed in no hurry to enter the hotel, walking around for quarter of an hour, surveying the place, obviously suspecting an ambush. Finally, he entered the hotel and a moment or two later, the receptionist rang Deirdre to say a visitor, a Mr Wilson, had come to collect Miss Heredia. Deirdre asked the hotel clerk to show the man to her room. "I'm scared stiff," she whispered to Maclean.

Already he and Pearson were taking up their positions, the detective behind the door and the psychiatrist in the bathroom. No sooner had they hidden than a knock came at the door. "Come in," Deirdre quavered.

As soon as the man entered, Pearson gave him no chance to say or do anything; he banged the door shut and sprang at him, wrapping his big arms round him and pinioning him. Maclean quickly searched the man. Plunging into an inside pocket, he emerged with a small automatic pistol in his hand.

"I have a licence for that," the man muttered, inconsequentially.

"We'll try to remember that," Pearson said, snapping handcuffs on the man's wrists.

Maclean was scanning the man's face. It fitted Maria's description of the man who had twice attacked her, down to the wine-stain birthmark in front of the left ear. Removing the trilby hat, the psychiatrist studied the hair, greying at the temples; somehow it did not match the face with those dyspeptic lines. Reaching round the man's head, Maclean gripped the edge of the hair and tugged, stripping off the wig and revealing a balding, greying head underneath. He peered at the birthmark, chiding himself for having missed it first time. From the man's coat pocket, Maclean produced a leather spectacle case containing bifocals; these he pushed on to the man's face while Pearson, Deirdre and the two detectives, who had entered the room, watched fascinated. "Dr Michael Barnes, isn't it?" the psychiatrist murmured.

"He'd have fooled me," Deirdre said, staring at the eyes behind the glasses. "When we met him, he had brown eyes."

"He still has," Maclean remarked. He turned to the man. "Everything's a bit blurred and a bit big with two sets of lenses to look through, isn't it, Dr Barnes?"

"Contact lenses," Deirdre exclaimed.

"A pair of the special kind with tinted irises that he ordered for his friend, Matthew Whittaker, aren't they, Dr Barnes?"

"I don't know what you are talking about," Barnes snapped.

"Where did you get the tip-off that Maria Heredia was here – from your brother-in-law?" Maclean asked. Barnes glared at him.

"His brother-in-law?" Pearson put in.

Deirdre went and fetched one of the group pictures she had unearthed and handed it to Maclean; he pointed to the dark, pretty girl in probationer's uniform linking arms with Anne Maxton. "This is your wife, isn't it, Dr Barnes – Margaret Crowther she was there." Barnes said nothing.

"You mean Frank Crowther's sister," Pearson said.

"The woman you heard him talking to just over two

hours ago," Maclean replied.

"My wife had nothing to do with any of this," Barnes exclaimed.

"Then you admit you killed Mrs Matthew Whittaker, also known as Carolina Heredia," Pearson said.

"I admit nothing."

Pearson had picked up the phone and was dialling Scotland Yard to give them details of the arrest they had made. "You can put out an immediate arrest call on these three people – Margaret Barnes, Robert Randal Newcombe, Anne Maxton." He gave their addresses and the reason for their arrest then put the phone down.

"Haven't you forgotten somebody?" Maclean asked.

Pearson gave him a hard look, then shrugged. "I can't arrest Frank Crowther," he muttered. "If he's still there, which I take it he is, he'll get the message. It's up to him to do the right thing and give himself up."

Maclean turned to Barnes. "One thing intrigues me. How did you kill Carolina Heredia – by suffocation?"

"I don't know what you're talking about," Barnes said.

"Then let me tell you why you had to kill her," Maclean continued. "When Whittaker got himself into trouble and had to disappear for good, you fixed everything. Your wife knew Anne Maxton from their probationer days and she arranged with her boyfriend, Newcombe, to alter Whittaker's features for which you paid them a tidy sum which they added to the fat fee they squeezed out of Whittaker. After that all you had to do was corrupt your wife's brother – Detective-constable Frank Crowther as he was then. He planted all the evidence Whittaker had given you in the police files at the first fire he investigated where bodies where burned beyond visual recognition."

"You have a perfervid imagination, Dr Maclean," Barnes sneered.

Maclean ignored the remark. He went on: "Then Whittaker, now alias Heredia, turns up in London and tries to put the touch on you and your friends for money. You find out where he is staying, bribe the proprietress and your friend Dr Cardew gets him a convenient bed in the very hospital where Anne Maxton is working. She helped you switch the marked bottles on the anaesthetics trolley and doctor the fuse-box. You thought Philip Rothwell would take the blame without putting up a fight. Maxton helped you again, didn't she – by procuring the flat keys the second time you attempted to kill Maria Heredia."

"But why did he have to kill them?" Pearson put in. "What did Barnes have to lose that was so important if Whittaker had been exposed?"

"Tell him, Barnes."

Barnes grimaced and narrowed his strange, blue eyes. "I've got nothing to say until I see my lawyer," he muttered.

"It was drugs, wasn't it?" Maclean said. He turned to Pearson. "Whittaker took all that trouble to get himself declared dead because he'd been smuggling drugs into the Continent for years and supplying the British black market and the underworld. He went in for pep pills like purple hearts and drugs like yellow submarines that paid big dividends. But he knew this was an offence most countries would have extradited him for."

"Why is there nothing in our files about this?" the detective asked.

"You'd better tackle Crowther about that."

"And Barnes was in this racket with Whittaker?"

Maclean nodded. "But Barnes did the thing in style. He got himself a licence to make LSD for psychiatric hospitals but produced enough to supply a more profitable market – the drug-pushers. From LSD, cocaine and heroin he has made a sizable fortune."

"Were Cripps and Wrigley in on this?" Pearson queried.

"I don't know," Maclean replied. "But Barnes made the running and did all the juggling with the firm's books. Get a squad of your men to search his country mansion and his town house and you'll find enough illegal drugs to convict him and his wife – and probably the suitcases Carolina Heredia was carrying when he lured her to her death."

Pearson was going to pick up the phone again when Barnes suddenly shouted, "I told you my wife had nothing to do with any of that. She knew nothing – nothing."

Pearson turned to look at Barnes, keeping his hand on the instrument. "We can keep your wife out of it," he said. "But you know what that means – you talk now and you tell us everything."

Barnes nodded, dumbly.

TWENTY-TWO

When he had replaced the instrument after calling his sister, Crowther slid open a desk drawer to produce a bottle of Napoleon brandy and a tumbler which he half-filled with the amber liquor; a couple of gulps and he felt its fiery rasp constrict his throat and its heat spread through his chest and stomach. He buzzed a constable and sent him to buy two ham and cheese sandwiches and a flask of coffee. From the way things were shaping it might be a long night, so he rang his wife to say he would be late home. At twenty to eight, the information-room sergeant rang him. "They've arrested a man at Holland Lodge Hotel, sir," he said. "Name of Barnes. I thought I'd let you know with your interest in the case. They've asked us to put out a general arrest alert for Barnes's wife and two other people, a woman called Maxton, and a surgeon by the name of Newcombe. Do I put them on the blower, sir?"

"Yes, go ahead sergeant. And thanks."

Crowther poured the last of his coffee and spiked it liberally with brandy. So often had he envisaged this situation, though never seriously imagining it really occurring. For several minutes he sat, mute and immobile, sipping the strong mixture while meditating what to do. There weren't many alternatives. When he had made up his mind, he tidied his desk. His senior colleagues must find nothing unusual, nothing amiss next morning. He left all his reports in a locked drawer and finished dictating his comments on a racing-fraud investigation, timing the message to prove he had worked late that evening. Looking round the office, he checked everything, then paused to gaze for several moments at the photo of his wife and two boys now in their late teens and heading for good careers in law and architecture; he had taken that snap on their Rhineland holiday the year before. Locking his door, he caught the lift to the Yard entrance and handed the desk sergeant his key; he exchanged a bit of chat with the man who had entered the force around the same time as himself, asking after his wife and boy. Satisfied he had projected the image of a man without a care, Crowther walked down to the basement, threw his briefcase into the Rover 3000 and climbed in behind the wheel. Within quarter of an hour he had joined the motorway and was heading homewards; on the M 4, the car seemed to drive itself, tunnelling after its lights; like that beam cutting a hole in the darkness, his mind appeared to focus on a small area of his past. That day so long ago, twenty-one years ago, when his sister, Margaret, had come to see him, tearful, afraid. Her husband, Michael, and the two other partners in Whittaker Pharmaceuticals had run into bad trouble. They had caught their chairman, Whittaker, out cooking the firm's books and stealing a huge amount of money. They'd all be involved in the crash and, as a private company, they'd be responsible to their creditors. It would mean bankruptcy, ruin and a scandal that would wreck Michael's and her life. But if Whittaker agreed to take the blame, if he disappeared as he wanted to, if he surrendered some of the money he had embezzled in order to flee, they'd be able to bail themselves out of the hole and perhaps even salvage some of the company's assets. That was where he, Crowther, came in according to his sister. They had to make Whittaker's disappearance foolproof for he had made this a condition of this flight. Their only way of doing that was to have him certified officially dead so that the British and international police would call off any hunt for him. Cripps, Wrigley and her husband could fake everything – documents, medical records, material evidence. But they needed two things – a body that matched Whittaker's, and somebody to substitute their evidence and Whittaker's dental records for the dead man's. "Frank, you'll do it, won't you?" Margaret had pleaded. "For me?" Above the whine of the engine, he could hear her voice invoking their fondness for one another, even their dead parents, and depicting their ruin, hers and Michael's, if Frank failed to help them. Finally, he had broken his trust and ceded. He had to confess it had also served his own ends. With his gorilla body and gargoyle face what did he have going for him, a modest little detective-constable with a slum background, no money and no high-placed, string-pulling friends. It almost seemed fate had taken him to that fire in the Ladbrook Hotel where they had found a man of Whittaker's build charred beyond fingerprint, facial and any other normal form of recognition. It had been too simple to palm those records. And Barnes had given him a handsome present for his services – money that enabled him to cultivate the right contacts and choose the right wife. Only later did he discover that Barnes had duped him, that Whittaker and he had been supplying crooks with drugs. And that made him, Crowther, an accessory to a major crime. He had to compound his earlier lapse and sieve everything out of Whittaker's Yard file that mentioned drugs or hinted about his own part in the investigation of that fire.

Just before Slough, he turned off the motorway, circled most of the town and took the home road north. He'd been a fool. But who imagined Whittaker ever surfacing again in Britain? Who believed a man dying accidentally on a surgeon's table would make any sort of stir? Crowther had taken no part in this crime, but he knew about it and had said nothing. He had also pointed Barnes at Whittaker's widow, aware that he meant to murder her and intended to kill the daughter. How could he justify himself now? He was a

Scotland Yard chief and he had become an accessory to three murders involving his brother-in-law and his sister!

Had he done it more subtly! But John Pearson's friend, that psychiatrist, had played him, the brilliant sleuth, at his own game, landing him right in an elementary ambush. And he, poor mutt, had fallen for the oldest con trick – the marked fiver! He could envisage the bludgeoning headlines and the stares of his colleagues which unreeled before him like the cat's-eyes glittering in his swathe of white light on the country road. It was Margaret's problem all over again, only worse; it would finish those nearest him, his wife and boys, his relations; it would shock his friends and the millions who knew him by reputation and those who had never heard of him but had faith in Scotland Yard. He could never survive psychological torture like that. Maybe a good lawyer might plead he had been coerced through family ties, if not blackmailed, into committing a crime and betraying his trust, that his part in the plot had been minor. He did not agree. Morality and honesty were monolithic and indivisible. One crack and the edifice crumbled.

Half a mile before Farnham Royal, he stopped at a quiet spot to crawl beneath the front, near-side wheel and tear away the tube that carried the brake fluid to it.

Death pre-empted all other punishment – the scandal, the loss of respect and his job, the trial and the nightmare his family would live through, the prison sentence. Death would erase that. And the Yard always looked after its own. His car had developed a brake fault and he had come into a right-hand bend with no brakes and travelling a bit fast. One of those things. Maybe a few of his Yard friends would understand at first hand how he had been tempted and had fallen.

When he left Collum Green behind, he pressed hard on the accelerator and the big car boomed on the metalled surface, its lights ricocheting and splintering on the elm and ash trees bordering the country road. Sixty – seventy – eighty – eighty-five. With the speedometer needle edging upwards, it seemed in some curious way that everything around him was occurring in slow motion as though his life were clinging desperately to those final seconds, trying to postpone the ultimate act. Approaching the bend, Crowther gripped the steering-wheel tightly, then shut his eyes and spun it hard to the left. He felt his body vibrate and buckle with the shock and his head din with the crash. But he had only a moment of pain as the car crumpled against a tree and crushed him in a tangle of metal.

TWENTY-THREE

Chief Superintendent Crowther never figured in the Whittaker Case or the trial that made front-page headlines for more than a week. Nor did his sister, Margaret Crowther Barnes. In his evidence, John Pearson made no mention of the dead Scotland Yard chief; and if one or two of his senior colleagues wondered about his accident and perhaps linked it with the indictment of his brother-in-law on two murder charges and a dozen drug offences, no one looked further for the cause than a ruptured brake pipe and bad luck. Michael Barnes made a full confession to the murders and drug charges on condition that no charge was laid against his wife who, he maintained, had never played any part in faking Whittaker's death, his murder or the subsequent crimes. She knew nothing about his drug-running or any other misdeeds, he claimed. Barnes was given life imprisonment with the judge stipulating a minimum of twenty-five years in prison.

Alongside Barnes in the dock, Anne Maxton fought hard for her freedom, denying everything. Yet, she could not refute the fact she had persuaded Newcombe to operate on Whittaker after his disappearance and therefore recognized him when he arrived in hospital under the name of Heredia. Nor could she reject Barnes's deposition that he had given her cylinders bearing the wrong markings to place in Rothwell's anaesthetics trolley and had helped him doctor the fuse-box. Several witnesses had spotted her in the old theatre block the evening before Whittaker's death. Evidence from Rothwell and the taxi-driver suggested that she had provided Barnes with the keys to burgle the mews flat and attempt to kill Maria Heredia. All this convinced the jury of her guilt as an accessory to murder and her other crimes. She was sentenced to ten years' imprisonment. Her friend and lover, Newcombe, could only plead guilty to aiding and abetting a wanted man and was given nine months in prison. However, as he predicted, the General Medical Council struck him off the medical register, his friends deserted him and he had to forsake Harley Street and sell much of his property.

Cripps and Wrigley proved to the jury's satisfaction they had no part in the Whittaker Murders and the homicide charges were dropped; they also pleaded, successfully, they knew nothing about Whittaker's and

Barnes's drug racket; however, both admitted having participated in the plot to have Whittaker declared officially dead and for this they each received a suspended sentence of six months' jail.

Innocent victim of the plot, Philip Rothwell was rehabilitated in his old job and handsomely compensated by the hospital. At Maclean's insistence, the coroner removed his remarks and reprimand from the official record and published a press statement exonerating the anaesthetist. As Maclean had predicted, John Pearson was promoted to the rank of detective-inspector and given a district in west London.

On the evening following the end of the trial, Pearson arrived at Harley Street to take both the psychiatrist and Deirdre for a celebration dinner. Deirdre was ushering out their last patient, a well-fleshed but attractive lady in her thirties who wore an elegant straw hat over blond hair, a summer frock obviously cut by some high-class couturier, fashionable sandals and several bits of costly jewellery. Pearson turned to admire the woman as Maclean emerged from his consulting-room. "You ought to have touched your forelock to her, John," the psychiatrist said with a grin. "She helped us set Anne Maxton running."

"I've never clapped sight on her," Pearson said. "Who is it?"

"Mrs Algernon Woodruffe," Maclean replied. He described some of the lady's problems and how they had finally led her to Newcombe for a nose-bob which had some therapeutic purpose."

"He used her as a visiting-card," Deirdre said, accusingly. "One of his patients and he used her as a visiting-card!"

"Our interests coincided," Maclean said, blandly.

"She needed a nose-bob and I needed to throw a scare into Newcome or Maxton."

"But if she's still having treatment here, the nose-bob wouldn't seem to have cured her mental trouble," Pearson remarked.

"Normally it would have helped," Maclean said. "But it gave her such a turn to have been laid on the slab under the knife of a man with criminal connections who was convicted of aiding and abetting a wanted man that the experience has lit up a whole constellation of neuroses. So, we've got her for another year at least."

"Secretly she's thrilled to bits at having her throat cut by Newcombe and her dewlap removed," Deirdre said. "She's turned her little melodrama into her sort of visiting-card and dines out on the story twice a week."

"I would think Newcombe will have a hard job selling his Harley Street premises after what's happened," the detective commented.

"A hard job!" Deirdre cried. "It's sold, and they had half a hundred offers from top specialists for it." She stabbed a finger at Maclean. "I even had to stop him from making an early bid for the rooms."

"I don't believe it," Pearson said, looking hard at Maclean.

"Well, it would have boosted our trade," Maclean remarked. "Think of the patients who'd feign any illness, make any medical excuse and write fat cheques just to claim they were treated on the couch in the room where the famous criminal surgeon operated." He gave a wry smile, a shrug then said, "Well, it was a thought."

Harley Street was emptying its consulting-rooms and the Rollses and Bentleys were pulling away from the parking bays when their street bell rang. Deirdre had been waiting for it. She pressed the button to open the door, then conjured two bottles of champagne in an ice-bucket from the cupboard and five glasses. "It's Maria and Philip," she explained as she wrestled with the wire of the champagne cork.

"You sure two anti-drink pledges can stand that stuff?" Pearson asked.

"Gregor hates it and Philip can take it or leave it," she said. Her Irish voice dropped to a conspiratorial whisper. "It's a special occasion," she said. "They're getting engaged – but I'll let them break the news themselves."

"I suppose this is the outcome of your personal little plot, mavournin," Maclean said, tongue in cheek.

Deirdre rose to the bait. "It was you who threw them together, remember?"

"Only for the purpose of the investigation," he came back.

"Oh! you're impossible," she got out. "If you want to know, I warned Maria to stay away from a reformed addict or she might get addicted to him. Like me."

Maclean smiled and kept his mouth shut. For he always believed in leaving Deirdre the last word.

NORTH EAST of SCOTLAND LIBRARY SERVICE
14 Crown Terrace, Aberdeen